I couldn't believe what I was seeing. . . .

I leaned forward and peered through my bedroom window.

Outside, the once-dark night was now lit with a creepy phosphorescence. The snow-covered landscape glimmered bright neon blue. It reminded me of the glow cast by a lit-up swimming pool. It had the same kind of underwater shimmer.

But this light wasn't coming from a pool. It was coming from up above.

I looked up and felt my heart skip a beat.

A fixed circular pattern of intense blue lights was moving slowly through the sky. Too slowly to be a plane.

No way, I thought as a cold tingle ran down my spine. *It can't be possible. . . .*

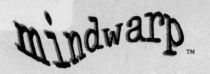

Alien Terror
Alien Blood
Alien Scream
Second Sight

Available from MINSTREL® Paperbacks

mindwarp ™

Second Sight

by
Chris Archer

A MINSTREL® BOOK

Published by POCKET BOOKS
New York   London   Toronto   Sydney   Tokyo   Singapore

A MINSTREL PAPERBACK *Original*

A Minstrel Book published by
POCKET BOOKS, a division of Simon & Schuster Inc.
1230 Avenue of the Americas, New York, NY 10020

mindwarp™ is a trademark of Daniel Weiss Associates, Inc.
Produced by Daniel Weiss Associates, Inc., New York

Copyright © 1998 by Daniel Weiss Associates, Inc.
Cover art copyright © 1998 by Daniel Weiss Associates, Inc.

ISBN: 0-671-01485-4

First Minstrel Books printing February 1998

10 9 8 7 6 5 4 3 2 1

A MINSTREL BOOK and colophon are registered trademarks of Simon & Schuster Inc.

Printed in the U.S.A.

Chapter 1

The sign was pink neon and shaped like the palm of a giant hand. Above it, a yellow neon eyeball blinked on and off.

MADAME MYSTERIA
CLAIRVOYANT
SHE SEES ALL
PSYCHIC READINGS $25

I'd been staring at it for about five minutes.

Behind me, the Metier Mall was pretty crowded for a Sunday. But it was the first weekend after New Year's, and a lot of people were here to return gifts and take advantage of the postholiday sales. My grandma Luisa was somewhere among

1

them, exchanging an ugly orange sweater she'd gotten from Uncle Hector. I was supposed to meet her in an hour by the main entrance. But for the next sixty minutes, I was on my own.

I could hear the other shoppers bustling past—chatting, laughing—headed on their way to the food court, or to the department stores, or to the movieplex, or maybe to the new laser-tag arena that had opened back in November.

On any other day, I might have joined them. But today was different. For one thing, it was the day before my thirteenth birthday. For another, it was the day I was finally going to do it.

I reached my hand into the pocket of my ski parka, feeling the crisp fifty-dollar bill that I'd found tucked into my stocking Christmas morning. "Buy yourself something special," Grandma Luisa had told me, giving me one of her winks.

Grandma knew that I had been wanting to visit Madame Mysteria ever since I'd first noticed the neon sign two months ago. Grandma also knew that twenty-five dollars was more money than I had saved up. But most of all, she knew my mother would never have let me spend my allowance visiting a psychic. Especially after the way Mom freaked out when she found out I called one of those psychic hot lines last month. (How was I to know it cost $3.99 a minute?)

No—Mom thought I should put all my money in the bank, just like she did when she was my age. She was always bragging about how, by the time she was seventeen, she had saved up enough money to buy her first car, and how—if I was smart—I would do the same.

That was the trouble with Mom.

It wasn't enough that I looked just like her, with the same straight black hair, boring brown eyes, and thick (horrible) eyebrows. She expected me to *be* just like her as well. She was even talking about which medical school I should attend, as if it were already decided that I was going to be a doctor, too.

I suppose that's how we were most different.

Mom saw the future as something that you planned out, calculated, and then went and made happen.

I saw it as something mysterious and unknown that happened *to* you.

Mom liked her world neat and orderly, with everything in its proper place.

Me—I liked intrigue and surprises.

I realized I was still staring at the glowing

neon eyeball as it continued to flash on and off in the storefront window. A gauzy white curtain was pressed behind it so that you couldn't see what was going on inside.

It was definitely intriguing.

Mom would have hated it—if she'd known about it. But she wasn't going to know. Grandma's fifty had seen to that. Since only half of it would be spent seeing Madame Mysteria, I'd still have twenty-five dollars left to buy some practical present Mom would approve of. Like underwear or school supplies. That way my trip to the psychic parlor could stay my little secret.

Well, here goes nothing, I thought, taking a deep breath and pushing my way through the door.

Once inside, all sense of mystery vanished.

I found myself in a drab little waiting room. Plain gray wallpaper and carpet, with a couple of framed watercolor paintings of flowers on the wall.

Across from the entrance, a thick red velvet curtain hung in a wide doorway. It was drawn tightly shut.

I suppose back there's where Madame M. does her readings.

Besides myself, there was only one other

person in the waiting room: a middle-aged woman with brown hair and horn-rimmed glasses, sitting on a sofa against the wall. She was engrossed in a magazine and didn't even look up when I entered. I noticed more magazines fanned out upon a wooden coffee table.

What kind of magazines does a psychic subscribe to? I wondered. My mind instantly conjured images of obscure periodicals with names such as *Past Life Digest* or *Séance Monthly*—but scanning the selection I was disappointed to discover nothing more exotic than the current issues of *Time*, *Woman's Day*, and *Popular Science*.

Yawn.

Picking up January's *National Geographic*, I took a seat across from the woman in a large, comfortable easy chair.

For a couple minutes I tried reading the cover story, an article on emperor penguins, but for some reason I just couldn't concentrate.

Soft music was playing out of a speaker in the ceiling—the easy-listening version of a Whitney Houston ballad, all violins and harps.

Muzak? I thought with disgust. *This is* not *what I expected.*

Come to think of it, none of it was.

In fact, if it weren't for the glowing neon palm in the window, or the thick velvet curtain, you'd think we were waiting to see a dentist.

It was all so . . . *normal.*

Setting down my magazine, I turned my attention to the velvet curtain. At least *it* was sort of interesting.

What goes on back there? I wondered.

However ordinary things seemed out front here, I could only imagine what sort of freaky rituals were being performed behind those curtains. I'd read enough to know the sort of creepy things that went on in psychic parlors.

Was Madame Mysteria in the middle of a séance? Could she be in a trance, channeling the spirit of someone's long-dead ancestor? The thought gave me goose bumps.

And what's she going to look like?

Any second I imagined the curtain would part and from the shadows she'd appear:

First, a pair of hands with nails like ten crimson daggers would snake forth.

Then two green eyes would glint like emeralds in the darkness.

Then her head would emerge—her thick raven black hair tied back in a golden silk scarf.

Fixing me in her hypnotic gaze, her ruby lips would curl back, exposing jagged yellow teeth.

Finally, her thickly accented voice would hiss—"Are you here for a reading?"

The voice was soft and friendly, not a hiss at all, but it made me jump all the same.

I looked across from me to see that the middle-aged woman had placed her own magazine down. She was smiling at me with her hands folded neatly on her lap.

"Hmm? Oh, yeah," I said, smiling back.

For the first time I got a good look at her. She was pretty plain by most standards. Her mousy hair was pulled back in a bun, and she wore a charcoal gray skirt and baggy sweater over a cream-colored blouse. Her thick glasses made her pale blue eyes look big and watery. She wasn't wearing any makeup.

Probably some lonely librarian, I figured. Here to ask Madame Mysteria whether she'll ever find a husband, or for advice on improving her love life.

If so, I had two words of advice for her myself: *contact lenses.*

"Is this your first time here?" I asked instead, trying to make some friendly small talk.

"First time?" the woman replied, sounding a

little confused. "Do you mean here in Metier? In that case, yes. I used to have a shop over in Milwaukee, but I'm afraid it didn't do too well. Too many skeptics, I suppose. But people seem much more into psychics in this town. I've only been in the mall about two months and business has been pretty steady."

My mouth had fallen open.

"You mean . . . *you're* Madame Mysteria?" I asked.

The woman grinned, pushing her glasses up on her nose. "At your service," she said. She rose, walking over to the curtain. "Shall we?" she asked.

I just stared at her, frozen in my chair.

"Is something wrong?" she asked.

"Oh no," I replied. "It's just that . . . you look so . . . I mean, I was expecting someone more, um . . ."

"Mysterious looking?" she finished for me. Her blue eyes twinkled.

"Well . . . *yeah*," I blurted. "I mean, from your name and all . . ." I pointed toward the flashing sign.

"Oh, *that*," she said, waving her hand in the air as if she were batting away an annoying insect. "I like to think of 'Madame Mysteria' as a kind of stage name. You know—something to help draw in the crowds."

"Then what's your real name?" I asked.

"Ruth Bogg," she answered, scrunching up her nose. "Doesn't have quite the same ring to it, though. Does it?"

I shook my head.

"And you are . . . ?" she asked, extending her hand.

"Elena," I said, shaking. Her grip was warm and firm. "Elena Vargas."

"Well, Elena," she replied. "Let's get down to business." She pushed aside the curtain and gestured inside. "After you."

Chapter 2

Beyond the curtain, Madame Mysteria's parlor was about the same size as the waiting room and (I was disappointed to discover) equally as boring.

The walls and carpet were more of the same dull gray. In the center of the room, a small round card table was surrounded by four wooden chairs. Madame Mysteria seated me in one, then seated herself in the chair opposite.

I looked around dejectedly.

Aside from a plain white tablecloth, the table was bare. No crystal ball. No tarot cards. Nothing.

Gee. She's a real no-frills psychic, I thought.

"I like to keep things simple," Madame Mysteria said, as if reading my mind.

Hey, I thought, perking up a little, *maybe she did just read my mind*.

Across from me, Madame Mysteria took off her glasses. She began wiping the lenses with a tissue from her sweater pocket.

"Elena . . . ," she said. "That's a very pretty name."

"Thanks," I replied.

"And yet . . . it's strange, but I'm sensing there's a different name for you . . . a nickname, maybe?"

I nodded. "My grandmother, Luisa, calls me *Milagrita*. It means 'little miracle' in Spanish."

"Ah, that must be it," Madame Mysteria said. "She is very close to you, your grandmother?"

"Yes," I said. "She lives with me and my mother."

"She is your mother's mother."

"That's right," I replied. "She's my only grand-parent now, since her husband—Grandpa Nico—died last year." I paused. "My father didn't have any . . . I mean, his parents died when he was a boy, so I never knew them."

As I spoke, I absentmindedly played with my watchband. It was one of those springy metal kinds, the type that can catch your arm hairs if you're not careful.

I often did this when I thought of my father.

The watch had belonged to him. Now it was mine. It was big and clunky on my wrist, but I wore it everywhere. Always had, ever since I was four years old. That was the year that Dad—

"It's because of him, isn't it?"

I looked up, to see Madame Mysteria had replaced her glasses and was studying me intently.

"*He's* the reason you're here," she said. She leaned across the table. "You want to know about your father."

I felt a lump form in my throat. I swallowed it down. "That's right. How did you know?"

"It is my job to know," she said simply. "He has been gone for a while," she added.

It wasn't a question.

"Yes," I said softly. "Over eight years."

"And you miss him," she said.

"Yes," I said, my voice now a mere whisper.

"Well, I have news for you, Elena," Madame Mysteria said, taking hold of my hands. "He misses you, too."

It took a second for her words to sink in.

"You mean . . . he's alive?"

The psychic stared into my eyes. It felt as if

she were looking straight into my soul. Then her gaze fell to my wrist.

"This is his, isn't it?" she said, indicating the watch.

I nodded.

"May I?" Madame Mysteria gently slid the timepiece over my hand. She held it cupped in one palm, then placed her other hand over it. She drew it to her chest.

"Ohhhhh," she said, moaning softly. "This watch gives off a strong energy."

I watched, spellbound, as Madame Mysteria placed my father's watch on the table. She passed her hands over it, as if she were warming them over a glowing coal. She seemed to enter some sort of trance. Her eyelids began to flutter and her crystal blue eyes rolled up toward the ceiling. When she next spoke, her voice sounded strange. Kind of deep and raspy.

"Your father . . . *is* alive, Elena. He misses you and wants to come home to you. . . ."

I clutched the edge of the table.

"Where is he?" I said. "Can you see him?"

"Not far . . . ," Madame Mysteria responded. "Not far . . . but he needs help finding his way."

14

"What kind of help?" I pleaded. "What can I do to help him?"

Madame Mysteria clapped her hands together loudly, making me jump. Her eyes focused on me again. "I think I have just the thing."

Rising, she scurried into a back room. A second later she returned, clutching something in her hands. Whatever it was, she handled it as if it were extremely fragile. She placed it carefully upon the table.

It was a cylinder of black wax, about as thick around as my wrist. I thought I detected the faint smell of licorice about it.

"A candle?" I said.

"Not just any candle," she replied. "This candle is very precious, Elena. One of a kind. It has been charged with very specific psychic energy. If you light it and place it in your window for seven nights in a row, it will help guide your father on his way home."

"Really?"

I leaned in to examine the candle more closely. Suddenly it didn't seem like such an ordinary candle anymore. I could almost feel a weird kind of energy coming out of it.

"Is it expensive?" I asked.

Madame Mysteria eyed me over the table. "I assure you, it's priceless," she answered. "And yet money is of no concern to me. I've had offers for hundreds of dollars. Thousands. But it's more important that I place the candle with its proper owner. Someone who truly has use for it. Someone who truly *believes*."

Almost without thinking, I pulled the fifty-dollar bill out of my pocket. "Here," I said, surprised at the desperate note in my voice. "It's not a lot, but it's all that I have." I slid the money across the table toward her. "Please, Madame Mysteria. I *do* believe. Honest. Let me have the candle," I begged.

The psychic regarded me for a few seconds. Then she smiled. "You have yourself a deal." She picked up the bill and tucked it in her sweater pocket. "I had a feeling you were the one."

I glanced at my father's watch, still lying on the table. It was five minutes to six.

"Oh, my gosh," I said, scooping it up. "I have to be going."

Madame Mysteria was already placing the candle in a paper bag with a small sheet of paper.

"Just follow the instructions," she said, handing the bag to me. "For seven nights."

16

"Seven nights," I repeated, heading toward the velvet curtain. "Thank you, Madame Mysteria."

"You're welcome," she answered, holding the curtain open. "And good luck to you."

I crossed through the waiting room, pushed my way out of the psychic's shop—

And walked straight into trouble.

"Trouble" had two heads, four legs, and enough makeup on to paint a small barn.

"Do you see what I see?" Sharon Flood said.

"I sure do," Monica Myers answered.

Sharon is blond and blue-eyed, captain of the Metier Junior High swim team, and one of the most popular girls in the seventh grade. Monica could have been her brunette, green-eyed twin. The two girls dressed alike, and sounded alike, and did everything together. For this year's talent show, they even sang a duet of "Wind Beneath My Wings."

And the sick part is, they actually won.

I guess they had a lot of people fooled.

Most of the girls at school would have killed to be their friend, but not me. I'd seen the way they treated some of the other "uncool" kids—as if anyone who didn't spend a fortune on clothes and hair-care products was beneath them.

17

The two girls walked up to me, wearing matching smirks.

"Don't tell me you just blew twenty-five bucks having your fortune told," Sharon said, snapping her chewing gum.

"What if I did?" I answered. "It's really none of your business."

"I know," Sharon said. "It's just that *I* could have told you your future for free."

Monica giggled, as if this were some great joke.

"Oh, really?" I said.

"Sure. Watch."

Sharon placed one hand lightly on my shoulder and brought her other hand up to her forehead. She closed her eyes and pretended to concentrate. "Yes . . . yes . . . I'm getting a premonition," she said in this fake spooky-sounding voice. "I can see . . . I see that you . . . are about to go . . . on a trip."

I suppose I should have seen it coming.

Suddenly Sharon's grip on my shoulder got stronger. She gave me a little shove, hardly enough to knock me down. But before I knew it, I was off my feet, tumbling backward through the air and landing hard on my butt.

Then I saw why.

Mick Myers, Monica's older brother, had been crouched on his hands and knees, right behind me. Now he was kneeling in front of me. Mick was an eighth-grader and on the boys' wrestling team. He, Sharon, and Monica were all cracking up.

"You sure *fell* for that one," Mick said, rising to his feet.

Some other day, I might have been upset.

Some other day, I might even have cried, or fought back, or worse.

But today I had other things on my mind. More important things.

I got up off the floor, picking up my bag and brushing off the back of my jeans.

"Gee, that was real mature," I said.

Then I turned and walked away, ignoring the mocking laughter that followed me through the mall.

Chapter 3

The first thing I did when I got home was light my candle.

According to Madame Mysteria's typewritten instructions, the candle's power worked best if you placed it near an item of the person who was missing.

I took my father's watch off my wrist and slid it around the candle. It was a perfect fit.

I set the candle in the middle of my windowsill.

Then, using one of the long fireplace matches from the tinder box downstairs, I lit the candle.

It gave off a wonderful sweet aroma.

Satisfied that the flame was burning brightly, I hurried out of my room to tell my mother the good news.

"Mom, I have something important to tell you," I said, rushing into the kitchen.

My mother was talking on the phone. When she saw me, she held up her finger.

I stopped in my tracks.

She cupped her hand over the mouthpiece. "Just a moment," she whispered. Then she spoke back into the phone: ". . . And how far apart are they, Mr. Gunderson?"

My mother's an obstetrician. That's the kind of doctor that delivers babies. She's always getting calls at odd times, sometimes in the middle of the night. This was the third call this weekend from Mr. Gunderson.

I plopped down in one of the kitchen chairs. We have the swiveling kind. As my mother continued her conversation, I pushed off the kitchen table, twirling myself around and around, faster and faster.

"Uh-huh," Mom was saying. "Uh-huh. Okay, Mr. Gunderson. There's nothing to worry about. I'll meet you and your wife at the hospital in half an hour."

I was putting on some serious speed. I found that by tucking in my legs, or by sticking them out, I could vary my rate of spin.

"I'll see you soon, too, Mr. Gunderson. Good-bye." Mom hung up the receiver. "Elena, *please*," she said, sounding weary.

I placed a sneaker on the floor. With a shrill *squeeeeeak*, the chair jerked to a halt. For a second, the world around me continued to tilt and whirl.

"I wish you wouldn't do that," Mom said, crossing to the back door. To my dizzy brain, it looked as if she were walking across the lurching deck of a ship. She plucked her white doctor's coat from its peg on the wall.

"That was Mr. Gunderson," Mom explained, as if I hadn't just heard her say his name a zillion times.

"Again?" I said.

"Yes." Mom sighed, buttoning her coat. "Except this time it sounds as if his wife is finally ready." She looked distracted. Her eyes scanned the kitchen, looking for something, then landed next to me.

She stepped toward me, scooping her pocketbook off the kitchen table.

"Mom, I need to—" I began. But she cut me off.

"There's some chicken and rice in the oven," she said, unzipping her pocketbook and fishing

23

around inside for her car keys. "And some banana pudding for dessert." She nodded toward the refrigerator.

"Mom, you won't believe what—"

"Oh!" Mom exclaimed, slapping her forehead. "I completely forgot to feed Felix. Could you do it, darling? There's still half a can of food left over from this morning, but be sure you put some dry food on top. Otherwise he doesn't—"

"—Dad's alive!" I blurted, standing up.

Mom froze, one hand still inside her pocketbook. As I watched, the color seemed to drain from her face. Her skin became as white as her doctor's coat.

". . . What?" she whispered.

"Dad's alive," I repeated. "And he misses us and wants to come home." I could barely contain my excitement. "Isn't that great news!"

My mother's pocketbook crashed to the floor.

In two swift steps she was across the kitchen. She seized hold of my arms. Her brown eyes peered deeply into mine.

"I don't understand," she said. "Did you . . . did you *see* him?" Her voice sounded strange. Lower than usual. Hoarser. And something else.

She sounded frightened.

24

"No . . . ," I said.

"Then how do you know these things?" she demanded. Her grip on my arms grew tighter.

Now *I* was frightened, too.

"B-because M-Madame Mysteria told me," I stammered.

"Madame Mysteria? Who is that?"

"She's—she's a psychic. Over at the mall." My voice was shaking.

Why is Mom reacting like this?

For a second, my mother continued to stare at me with a scared look in her eyes. Then, slowly, her grip relaxed on my arms. She shook her head slowly.

When she spoke again, she didn't sound scared anymore.

She sounded angry.

"So . . . a *psychic* told you your dead father was still alive. And *you* believed her."

My mother let go of my arms, then waved her hands at the ceiling. "Oh, Elena! How can someone as smart as you sometimes be so foolish?"

"But . . . but Madame Mysteria told me—"

"—what you wanted to hear," Mom interrupted. "She told you what you wanted to hear. That's what they do, these so-called 'psychics.'

25

They look in their crystal balls and they tell you their lies, and then they take your money."

"But Madame Mysteria isn't like that," I protested.

"Oh, so I suppose she gave you a reading for free?"

"No," I admitted, looking down at my feet. My cheeks were burning.

My mother sighed loudly. "I'm not even going to *ask* how much you paid her." She glanced at her watch. "I'm going to be late for the hospital."

She headed for the back door. "We'll talk about this tomorrow, young lady."

Grandma Luisa stepped into the kitchen next to me. "What's going on here?" she asked, her eyes flashing with concern.

I was too upset to speak. I just stood there, trembling.

"Mercedes?" Grandma said, looking toward my mother. "What's the matter?"

"What's the matter," Mom said, "is that tomorrow your granddaughter will be turning thirteen, and yet she still wants to believe in fairy tales."

"They're not fairy tales!" I yelled. I rushed out of the kitchen, pushing past my startled grandmother. "They're not!"

I ran up the stairs and to my room as hot tears spilled down my cheeks.

I must have cried into my pillow for about ten minutes before I heard the door to my bedroom open and soft, tentative footsteps pat their way over to my bed. I felt the mattress sag as someone sat down next to me. I didn't have to look up. I could tell who it was by her rose-scented perfume.

"*Milagrita, Milagrita,*" Grandma Luisa said, lightly stroking my hair. "Don't be crying so."

I rolled over onto my back and gazed up into my grandma's eyes. They were as deep brown as chestnuts and glistened in the light from my bedside lamp. For a moment, I was struck by how closely she resembled my mother.

"You know," she continued, "they have a saying in Mexico: 'You must save your tears for the sad times.'"

"But I *am* sad," I told her, sniffling.

She smiled, shaking her head slowly. "No," she said, tweaking my chin. "You are angry. Angry because your mother doesn't share your point of view. But you should have learned by now: We are a house of stubborn women."

27

"But why did Mom get so upset?" I asked.

Grandma Luisa tilted her head, considering my question. I noticed she was holding something in her lap. A book of some sort.

"I think she is worried because you are growing to be so much like your father."

As she spoke, she ran her hands lightly across the book's cover, stroking it as if it were a cat. Then she glanced down at it, as if she were surprised to find it in her hands.

"*Ay!* How silly. I almost forgot . . . here."

She handed the book to me.

Sitting up, I examined the volume more closely.

It looked old. Its cover was of rich brown leather that was peeling away at the edges. There might have been a title printed on it once, but all that remained were some flecks of gold lettering on the spine. I looked up at my grandma with a curious expression.

"Go ahead," she said. "Open it."

I did, and was instantly overtaken by a thick, musty odor. It made me want to sneeze. Crinkling my nose, I noticed a name printed in ink in small, neat letters across the top of the inside cover: E. Vargas.

"It was Emilio's," my grandma explained.

Dad's?

A tingle of excitement crept up my arms. I turned a yellowed leaf and read the title page:

EXPLORATIONS IN THE PSYCHIC REALM
A Manual for the Mind's Eye

"You see," Grandma went on, with a twinkle in her eye, "you are not the first 'E. Vargas' to believe in psychic power."

"You mean . . ."

Grandma Luisa nodded. "Your father was always reading this book. So many nights I would see him sitting in his chair, that book open in his lap, with a look on his face like he was a million miles away." She smiled at the memory.

My mind was reeling. *My father was into the supernatural, too?*

"How come I never saw this book before?" I asked.

My grandma's smile faded.

"After the accident, your mother gave away most of your father's things—his books, his clothes," she said. "She said it was to make room, but it was as if she were destroying all traces of him. I think it was because she couldn't bear to be reminded of the tragedy. Still, I couldn't let her get rid of this book. It was so special to him. I've been keeping it to give to you, *Milagrita*."

She brushed a strand of hair out of my face, stroking my cheek.

"Your father was always talking about the future, and of *your* future—about how proud you were going to make him someday. He seemed so sure of the things he said—it was as if he had seen it all already, or could predict it somehow. He could always tell when a storm was coming, or when someone would be having a baby. When people asked him how he knew these things, he claimed he had *El Visión Segundo*—'Second Sight'—the ability to foresee the future. He even had your mother convinced, which is no small feat, I can tell you."

My grandma chuckled at the thought. Then her expression darkened.

"That is why the accident came as such a shock to her. If your father *was* psychic, as he claimed, then why didn't he see it coming? Where was the mystical power to warn him to stay off the road that day? Why didn't he save himself?"

"But maybe he *did* save himself, Grandma," I said, leaning toward her.

My grandma clucked her tongue.

"There were witnesses, Elena," she said. "People saw your father's car skid off the road and over the cliff. They saw the explosion."

"Yes, but the police never recovered his body. You told me that yourself."

"They say it could have been destroyed in the fire."

"*Could* have been," I said. "But maybe not."

My grandma nodded sadly. "'Maybe not.' That's just what your mother said. For almost a year after the accident, she kept hoping your father might walk back through the front door. But he didn't, and she lost that hope. That's why it upsets her to see *you* get so excited. She doesn't want you to be hurt the way she was."

She got up from my bed. "It's getting late. I should feed poor Felix." She started crossing toward the door.

"Do you think my father's dead, Grandma?" I said.

My grandma paused in the doorway.

"They have an expression in Mexico," she said. "'We are alive as long as we are loved.'"

She turned to me. "I think your father is alive in your heart. And I think he would have wanted you to have that book."

*   *   *

31

That night, I stayed up reading my father's book.

It was set up like a textbook. Each chapter described a different kind of extrasensory perception, or ESP. There were sections on mind reading, palm reading, something called "divining"—and then exercises for the reader to practice them with.

My father's small, neat handwriting was crammed in the margins of almost every page. In some parts he had underlined entire paragraphs. It looked like the excited scribbles of a nerdy schoolboy.

Gosh, he really was *into all this stuff.*

One chapter was titled "Psychometry." It was all about the psychic ability to receive extrasensory perceptions about a person by touching a personal item of his or hers.

Hey, I realized, *that must be what Madame Mysteria did with Dad's watch.*

I flipped through some more, when a particular passage caught my eye.

Candles
The use of candles as a psychic instrument has been well documented, and dates back as far as the twelfth century A.D.

32

By concentrating on the pure light of a candle flame, the psychic is thus able to clear his or her mind, and enter a dreamlike state.

In this dream state, sometimes called a "fugue" or "candle trance," time seems to stand still. The psychic can receive premonitions of the future, as well as commune with the spirit of another psychic.

The clock in the hallway started chiming midnight.

I stopped reading as a strange flickering light played across the page. I looked up from the book toward the bedroom window.

On the sill, the candle flame was sputtering—flapping, almost—as if it were being blown in a gentle but steady breeze. Maybe there was a draft seeping in from outside.

Placing my book facedown on my nightstand so I wouldn't lose my place, I threw back the comforter and crossed the room toward the window. As I approached, the candle began flickering more violently, as if the draft it was in were getting stronger. I could even hear it making a sound, a soft *ffp-ffp-ffp-ffp-ffp*. . . .

Just as I reached the window, the flickering stopped.

The candle burned strong and evenly.

That's weird.

Lifting the candle off the sill, I ran my free hand slowly along the bottom and sides of the window, tracing all along the cracks. I couldn't feel a thing.

No chilly draft, no hint of an air current whatsoever.

I placed the candle back on the window ledge, frowning.

So, if not a draft, what had caused the flickering before?

Maybe it's just a defective candle, I thought, staring at the bright yellow-white flame. *Too bad it's one of a kind. Otherwise I could take it back to Madame Mysteria's and ask for anoth*—

My thoughts were interrupted as an eerie blue light suddenly illuminated the entire windowsill.

For a second I thought it was the candle acting weird again. But then it hit me—

The light was coming from *outside*.

Sliding the candle over, I leaned forward and peered through the window, pressing my hands sideways against the glass to cut the glare from inside my room.

Outside, the once-dark night was now lit with

a creepy phosphorescence. The snow-covered landscape glimmered bright neon blue. It reminded me of the glow cast by a lit-up swimming pool. It had that same kind of underwater shimmer.

But this light wasn't coming from a pool. It was coming from up above.

I looked up and felt my heart skip a beat.

A fixed circular pattern of intense blue lights was moving slowly through the sky. Too slowly to be a plane.

No way, I thought as a cold tingle ran down my spine. *It can't be possible. . . .*

Chapter 4

A UFO! I'm finally seeing one for myself.

My hometown—Metier, Wisconsin—is kind of famous for being a "UFO hot spot." There have been so many sightings of strange lights in the sky that some residents even want to change the town's name to "Meteor." I always thought the stories about aliens and flying saucers were bogus— until this very minute.

Now I was staring at proof.

Whatever the object was, it must have been almost directly over our house before, but now it was heading away, moving off over the woods that bordered on our backyard. As it retreated into the distance it tossed crazy, shifting shadows on the flat snow.

It was getting harder to see through the window—my breath was steaming up the glass.

I used the cuff of my flannel pajamas to wipe away the condensation. Once it was clear, I peered out again—

And gasped.

Because someone was in my backyard.

A man.

Had he been there all this time? I'd been too busy looking at the sky before to notice.

Although I should have been frightened, for some reason I wasn't. The man seemed oddly familiar to me somehow.

And he was just standing there. Standing in the snow. Staring up at my window.

At my candle.

I tried to look closer. He was too far away to see clearly, but I could tell he was tall and thin, with dark hair.

Could it be . . .

"Dad?" I said, placing my palm against the window. My voice was a mere whisper.

The man turned away and started walking into the woods. In the same direction as the UFO.

"Dad!" I yelled louder, this time knocking on the glass. "Hey! Don't go!"

If he heard me, he showed no sign of it. He just kept walking away across the snow, as if in a trance.

It's him. It has to be.

Before I knew what I was doing, I picked up the candle from the window ledge and rushed out of my room, pausing only to slide my feet into the pair of fuzzy slippers sitting by my door.

I hurried along the dark hallway, hearing Grandma Luisa's loud snoring as I passed her bedroom. For a second I debated waking her, but decided there wasn't any time to waste.

I quickly descended the back stairway into the kitchen. Then, twisting the lock open, I headed out the back door and into the night.

Immediately, my heart sank.

The backyard was empty. There was no one in sight.

Had I imagined the whole thing?

No—I could just make out a set of footprints leading into the woods.

I started trudging across the snow in my slippers. I'm sure it was freezing out, but I barely noticed. My entire body felt flushed with a weird excitement. Plus, aside from giving off light, the candle in my hand seemed to radiate a decent amount of heat.

I followed the footprints into the woods. They were big and wide, and I found that by tracing them, step for step, travel through the foot-deep snow was made easier. So, using the footprints as my guide, I soon was moving quickly through the barren trees.

Though I had been in these woods hundreds of times before, it had always been during the day. Now, in the moonlight, the forest was completely unfamiliar to me. If it weren't for the tracks in the snow, I wouldn't have known which way to go, and worried that I'd never find my way back.

I hadn't gone far before I noticed more strange blue lights shining in the distance. But rather than coming from the sky, these lights seemed to be shining from ground level, several hundred yards up ahead. As I watched, I thought I could detect the man, a mere shadowy silhouette in the distance. Encouraged, I quickened my pace.

After another couple minutes, I came into a clearing, and froze in my tracks. I finally saw where the lights were coming from. And my mind reeled at the sight.

There, in the middle of the field, stood a gleaming metal craft. It was huge and circular—perfectly smooth—and maybe twenty feet in diameter. I figure it must have given off an awesome amount of heat when it landed, for the snow underneath the craft had melted away in a perfect circle, exposing the dead, matted grass beneath.

Six delicate, spindly legs held the main body suspended about ten feet above the ground, as a ring of blue lights pulsed in a steady rhythm on its underside, like a heartbeat.

It seemed alive somehow. Like a giant silver beetle.

Alive . . . and waiting. But for what?

Then I saw the man.

He was standing almost directly underneath the craft, in the center of the grassy clearing. Though he was facing away from me, I was practically certain it was my father.

I started to wave and was about to call to him when a loud humming noise filled the air.

As I watched in awe, a brilliant white line appeared on the underside of the craft. It started to spread, to grow wider, and I realized that it was a kind of hatchway opening up. A ramp descended from the rectangular opening. Inside the craft, the light was blinding. It poured out onto the ground like a spotlight.

The man started to walk up the ramp into the light.

The humming was growing louder. Along the perimeter, the blue lights began flashing faster and brighter, in a circular sequence. As they flashed dizzily, they seemed to stir up a breeze. All around the craft, powdery snow began to kick up in whirling, spidery drifts.

It's going to take off, I realized. For some reason, the thought panicked me and snapped me into action.

Shielding my candle flame with my hand, I started running toward the humming ship.

I can't let him get away. I can't lose him. Not again.

I reached the metal ramp just as it started rising back into the craft. I jumped upon it, riding it up through the rectangular hatchway.

The light from above was so powerful, I had to squint my eyes as I was raised inside the craft, finally shutting them altogether. Even with my eyes shut, I could see the light, glowing hotly upon my eyelids. I felt the ramp come to a stop, then heard a gentle *whoosh* as the hatchway slid shut. At once, the loud humming from outside was cut off.

There was utter silence. The light against my eyelids faded.

Blinking back tears, and not knowing what I'd see, I opened my eyes.

It took a couple seconds for my eyes to adjust.

I was standing in the middle of a kind of control room. The walls were lined with a vast array of strange-looking computers. Their glowing screens cast the only light into the cubicle.

The man I'd followed was standing before one of the monitors, his back to me.

Stepping down off the ramp, I crossed over toward him. With every step, my heart pounded in my ears.

"Dad . . . ?" I said hesitantly.

The man didn't turn around. Had he heard me?

I took a step closer.

"It's me . . . Elena."

This time, he cocked his head slightly.

I reached out a trembling hand and was about to touch his shoulder, when a sharp, incredible throbbing sensation tore through my head.

I gasped, wincing in pain—

And when I opened my eyes, I was standing back in my bedroom, staring at the candle burning on my windowsill. It was flickering, making a soft sputtering sound: *ffp-ffp-ffp-ffp-ffp*.

Then it stopped, burning evenly again.

I was completely disoriented. What was going on here?

My eyes darted frantically around my room.

My father's watch read 12:02 A.M.

My slippers were resting next to the door. Fluffy and dry.

I rushed to my bed. My father's book was lying facedown on my nightstand, right where I'd placed it.

I put a hand on my mattress. It was still warm with body heat.

A shiver ran down my spine.

I had imagined it all. The strange lights, the man, heading into the woods, the spaceship. Everything.

With trembling legs, I climbed back into bed, pulling my comforter up to my chin.

What just happened to me?

My gaze fell to my father's book.

I had a sudden scary thought:

Had I just experienced a "candle trance"?

If so, was everything I'd just seen a premonition of things to come?

Was I going to meet my father?

Chapter 5

I awoke the next morning with the memory of the previous night's experience still clear in my mind. I was convinced that what I had seen and gone through had been a real psychic premonition.

As I looked in the mirror and brushed my teeth, I became even more certain that my father and I had a deep spiritual connection. Last night had been his way—on the eve of my birthday—of trying to contact me.

The more I thought about it, the more answers rushed to my mind.

Elena Vargas, you are thirteen and you have El Visión Segunda!

I smiled at myself in the mirror and decided to take my father's book with me to school.

The best part of a gift—even if the gift is psychic ability—is sharing it with your friends.

"Hurry up, *Milagrita*. The school bus is waiting for you!" My grandmother's voice called up from downstairs.

Sure enough, I heard the honk of the bus outside my window and rushed out into the hall. Grandma Luisa met me on the landing.

"You know what they say in Mexico," she said, holding out my lunch bag. "'Be late on your birthday, and you'll be late the whole year long.'"

I took my lunch from her. "You know what, Grandma? Sometimes I think you make these sayings up."

"Perhaps . . . ," she said. She gave me a sly wink. "Perhaps not."

I kissed her on the cheek, then scurried down the rest of the stairs and ran toward the front door.

"*Feliz cumpleaños*, Elena," she called after me.

"*Gracias, Abuela*," I called back. I reached for the doorknob—

And a sudden rush of dizziness overcame me.

It was similar to the feeling I'd had last night, spinning in the kitchen chair, only a hundred times stronger. It made my knees shake.

Reaching out behind me to steady myself, I grabbed hold of the umbrella stand that stood by the front door. I took a slow, even breath and tried to concentrate on shaking off the dizziness.

Then, as suddenly as it had arrived, the dizzy spell ended.

Whoa. That was weird, I thought.

The bus honked once more and I rushed out to meet it.

"Hey, Elena," a voice called out to me as I reached my locker.

I turned to look, but in the massive throng of students walking down the hall I couldn't make out who it was.

Then I noticed the fedora hat bobbing through the crowd, headed my way.

It was Cleveland Coopersmith.

Even with the hat on, he was still the shortest kid in school.

"Did you make a wish last night?" he asked.

"Cleveland," I said, rolling my eyes. "My birthday is today. I didn't blow out any candles last night."

But I did light one, I added to myself.

"What are you talking about?" Cleveland

frowned and pulled his fedora down over his eyes. "I'm talking about the great big shooting star that flew through the sky last night. When you see a shooting star, you're supposed to make a wish. Don't you know that?"

"It wasn't a star. It was a UFO." The words crossed my lips before I had a chance to think clearly about what I was saying.

"A UFO?" Gary Beck's voice piped up behind me.

I turned.

Gary was the biggest science geek at Metier Junior High—a role he was proud of. "Don't tell me you're buying into that flying saucer nonsense," he said.

I blushed, slightly embarrassed. But I would not be deterred.

"I know what I saw, and it wasn't a shooting star."

"Oh, really?" Gary Beck challenged.

"Yeah. Really."

"And I suppose you fought off the tiny green men with your umbrella," Gary continued, laughing to himself.

"Huh?" I didn't understand what he meant.

Then Gary pointed.

I looked down and saw that I had one of the umbrellas from home held firmly in my hand. I must have grabbed it when I had that dizzy spell in the front hallway.

"You think it's going to rain or something?" Cleveland asked, joining Gary in a chuckle.

"Maybe I do," I snapped, defensively. "Why not?"

Cleveland stared at me blankly.

Gary came to his defense. "Because, Elena, it's January," he explained. "And it doesn't rain in Metier in January. It's far too cold. Precipitation in the form of rain would be meteorologically il-logical."

"Yeah," Cleveland said, nodding toward Gary. "That's just what I was about to say."

I have to admit, I was more than a bit con-fused. Why had I taken the umbrella? And how could I have come all the way to school and not even have noticed that I was holding it?

My thoughts were interrupted as the morning bell rang. I shoved the umbrella into my locker with my coat, then hurried to homeroom.

I got about fifty feet before I was rocked by an-other violent dizzy spell.

This one was even worse than the one I'd felt

earlier. My vision blurred. For a second, it felt as if the entire school were rolling down a hill.

I staggered against the wall, tripping over my legs, trying to regain my balance.

When my head stopped spinning, I realized I was leaning up against the door to one of the classrooms. I stared through the wire-enforced window in the door, trying to focus my eyes.

Slowly, the figure of Mr. Garfield, my math teacher, came into focus.

He was standing at the front of the room, writing something in big letters across the top of the blackboard: P-O-P Q-U-I-Z.

Mr. Garfield turned around briefly, and I noticed something odd about him. I couldn't quite place what it was, and then it hit me: He wasn't wearing one of his usual ugly bow ties.

As I watched, Mr. Garfield turned back to the board and started writing out problems. Problems with fractions.

Yikes, I thought. I had Mr. Garfield first period. And we hadn't studied fractions since the fall.

If he's going to give us a pop quiz, I thought, *I better review my notes.*

* * *

Entering homeroom, I took my seat in the front row, next to Toni Douglas. Taking my math book out, I flipped it open and began reviewing the chapter on fractions.

"Hey, El. What's up?" Toni asked when she saw what I was doing. "You look a little worried."

"Mr. Garfield is going to give a pop quiz in class today," I replied.

"Really?" Toni said. Her eyes widened. She had Mr. Garfield first period, too.

"Yeah. On fractions."

"Did you see that in your crystal ball?" sneered a voice.

"Or did one of your 'psychic friends' tell you?" scoffed another.

I looked up to see Sharon Flood standing directly over me. Monica Myers was standing beside her, as usual.

I swear, you'd think they were joined at the hip.

"No," I told them. "For your information, I just passed Mr. Garfield's room and saw him writing problems on the board."

"Well, for *your* information," Sharon shot back, "you're wrong."

Monica giggled.

I rolled my eyes. "Whatever you say, guys," I

said, turning back to my notes. "Don't say I didn't warn you."

Unfortunately for me, Sharon wasn't about to let up.

"First of all," she stated smugly, holding up one perfect pink-nail-polished finger, "Mr. Garfield *never* gives pop quizzes."

I sighed. "Well, there's a first time for everyth—"

"Second of all," Sharon interrupted, holding up another finger, "we studied fractions way back in October, so it doesn't make sense that Mr. Garfield would be testing us on them now."

"Maybe so, but—"

"And third of all, *I* just saw Mr. Garfield out parking his car in the teachers' lot, which means he hasn't even been to his room yet. Which *further* means that you're either a liar, or crazy, or both."

"Hmm . . . ," Monica said, crossing her arms and regarding me. "I'd say 'both.'"

"I know what I saw," I said.

"And *I* know what *I* saw," Sharon said.

I stared her right in the eye.

"I guess we'll just have to wait 'til first period to find out which of us is right," I said. "But until then, if you'll both excuse me, I have some study-ing to do."

"Go ahead, waste your time," Sharon said, tossing her blond hair over her shoulder. "We already know you waste your money."

With that, Sharon moved off to her desk in the back of the room. Monica followed, a half step behind.

When they had left, Toni Douglas leaned over to me.

"Sharon thinks she knows everything," she said softly. "I hope Mr. Garfield *does* give us a quiz, if only to shut her up for once."

"Oh, he'll give it to us," I added, sounding more sure of myself than I felt.

Inside, I was thinking about the strange episode I'd had last night, when I imagined following the man who looked like my father into the UFO.

Now it sounded totally crazy, but it had seemed so real at the time.

Just as real as seeing Mr. Garfield ten minutes ago.

I shuddered at an unpleasant thought: *Could I have imagined Mr. Garfield, too?*

*   *   *

Homeroom went by in a whir. All through the flag salute and the morning announcements, I kept one eye on my math notes and the other on the clock.

When the bell for first period finally rang, I sat frozen in my seat.

"Aren't you coming, Elena?" Sharon Flood snickered as she passed my seat. "Don't want to be late for that imaginary quiz, now, do you?"

Laughing, she and Monica exited into the hall-way.

For another full minute, I continued to sit motionless at my desk.

Soon the classroom was empty except for me and Mr. Blanchard, my homeroom teacher.

"Elena?" he said, frowning. "Are you okay?"

I suppose I must have looked a little spaced out.

"I'll know in a couple minutes," I said. Then, rising, I folded up my notebook, slung my book bag over my shoulder, and headed out the door.

The walk to first period seemed a million miles long. All the way, I felt as if I were floating—I could barely feel my feet hitting the ground. Around me, other kids were rushing to their own classes, talking and laughing. But it was as if they were all moving in slow motion. Their voices sounded strange and underwater to me.

And suddenly I was standing outside Mr. Garfield's room.

I closed my eyes. I wondered if you needed a cake and candles to make wishes come true on your birthday. I sure hoped not. Even so, I crossed my fingers for insurance.

"Please, let there be a quiz today," I whispered. "Please let me not look like an idiot in front of Sharon Flood."

Then, taking a deep breath, I stepped into the room.

I was the last kid to arrive. Everyone else was already at their desks.

Keeping my head down, I tried not to look at the blackboard as I made my way to my seat.

I didn't have to look. I could tell by the expression on Sharon Flood's face as I passed her desk.

She was grinning from ear to ear, like the Cheshire cat.

Plunking down in my chair, I finally braved a peek at the blackboard.

It was completely blank.

Not only blank, but washed clean. You can tell

if something's been written in chalk and then erased. This blackboard obviously hadn't been written on at all today.

I looked over toward Sharon. She was looking right at me. "I told you," she mouthed at me.

I sunk down in my seat.

It's bad enough finding out you're crazy. It's worse when other people know it, too.

The late bell rang.

At the front of the room, Mr. Garfield got up from behind his desk. "Class," he began, fidgeting with his bow tie, "being that it's a new year, a lot of people have made resolutions. Lose weight, stop smoking, start eating more green vegetables, and so forth. Well, I, too, have made some resolutions. For one, I'm going to stop wearing these ugly bow ties!" With a violent motion, Mr. Garfield ripped the tie from around his neck.

Around the room, several kids erupted in shocked laughter.

"My second resolution is one I'd like for us all to take part in. This year, I would like for us to reacquaint ourselves with old forgotten friends."

Mr. Garfield headed toward the blackboard.

For some reason, my heart started beating faster.

"I thought we'd start with some pals we made way back in October," Mr. Garfield said. "Namely, fractions. And I know just the way to do it."

He picked up the chalk, then started writing: P-O-P Q-U-I-Z.

A collective groan went up around the room.

"But, Mr. Garfield," Ben Jameson protested, "you never gave us a pop quiz before."

Mr. Garfield smiled. "That's another good thing about new years," he said. "They're a great time for turning over new leaves." Then, turning around, he started writing math problems on the board.

In the second row, Toni Douglas spun around and gave me a thumbs-up sign. I gave it back. My head was reeling.

I predicted this, I thought. *I actually saw into the future.*

I wasn't quite sure how that made me feel.

Then I noticed Sharon Flood.

She was staring at me. She looked stunned. Her jaw was hanging open.

I sat up a little taller in my seat.

"I told *you*," I mouthed at her defiantly.

I decided that it made me feel *good*.

Chapter 6

It didn't take long for news of my "psychic abilities" to get around school. I suppose Toni
Douglas must have spread the word, because I
know it wasn't Sharon Flood.

Sharon had been so shocked, I didn't think
she'd be able to talk at all for some time—much
less talk about *me*.

By the time lunch rolled around, I was practically world famous. All eyes were on me as I
strode into the lunchroom, my chin in the air and
my father's book tucked squarely under my arm.

For a minute after I took my seat, the other
kids at my table just stared at me. Then they all
started talking at once.

"So how'd you do it?"

"Fess up, Vargas."

"Are you really psychic?"

"C'mon. Did Garfield tell you about that quiz?"

"Can you actually see the future?"

I smiled mysteriously, gazing around the table at the group of boys before me.

For some reason, I was the only girl who ever sat at this table. I'm not sure why that was—it's just the way things worked out. Although, sometimes, from the way the others carried on, it seemed as if I were the only normal person who sat there, too.

"I suppose it might have something to do with the fact that it's my thirteenth birthday," I said. "You know what they say about thirteen being a magical number and all."

"Yeah, right," said Byron Prendergast, stuffing half his mouth with a meatball hero. "I'm thirteen, too, but *I've* never predicted the future."

"Yeah," said Leonard Dooley. "Me too. So that can't be it."

"Well," I said. "It might also have something to do with this book on psychic power, which belonged to my—"

Before I could finish, Cleveland Coopersmith

reached over and snatched the book from my hands.

"Hey!" I protested. "Give it back."

"I will, I will—in a minute," Cleveland said, flashing a wicked grin to the rest of the table. He opened the book and started thumbing through the pages. "After all, why should you be the only one to cash in on this psychic stuff?"

"Yeah, Vargas," Vinnie Carlucci said. "We could *all* be psychics. Then we could all know what problems are going to be on the math tests."

"Yeah," Nick Carlucci, Vinnie's twin brother, added. "Or when lunch lady Mulligan is going to serve her mystery meat loaf."

"And then hold a séance to see what it was in its past life," cracked Leonard Dooley.

"You guys are all thinking too small," Byron Prendergast said over a mouthful of potato chips. "I say, forget math tests and lunch meat. We should go to the racetrack and predict which horses are going to win. We could clean up!"

"No, we couldn't," Ben Jameson said. Ben was class president and perhaps the most rational guy at our table. "You have to be eighteen years old to gamble."

"No problem," Byron said, taking a swig of

chocolate milk. "We just get some grown-up to place the bets for us." Wiping his mouth, he turned to the red-headed kid at the far end of the table. "Hey, Jack, your stepfather's pretty cool, right?"

"Hmm? Oh yeah," Jack Raynes muttered. He was sitting directly across from me. Usually he was the most talkative of our bunch, but so far today he'd been oddly silent. And was it my imagination, or was he staring at me funny?

Perhaps my psychic powers have weirded him out, I thought. *That, or he's just jealous that for once he's not the center of attention.*

"See?" Byron said, growing excited. "We could use Jack's stepdad. Or maybe get old man Beister down at the mall. He'd *definitely* do it."

"Are you kidding?" Vinnie replied. "Can you see Mr. Beister at the racetrack? He'd probably spook all the horses!"

The rest of the table cracked up.

Ed Beister was kind of a joke around town—Metier's number-one Looney Tune. At one time he had been a famous lawyer or something, but something made him snap. Now he just roamed around the shopping mall, covered head to toe in tinfoil and mumbling to himself.

62

"So, Cleveland," Byron said. "Have you found out any good stuff yet?"

Cleveland looked up from my father's book, frowning. "I'm not sure. I mean, it's kind of like reading the encyclopedia."

"Well, give us a sample," Vinnie said.

"All right . . . ," Cleveland said. He flipped a page and began reading at random. "'While the average person views the world through only two eyes, the psychic views it through three. Using this *third eye*, the psychic is able to recognize phenomena outside of the normal visual spectrum. One such phenomenon is the *aura*, or life energy, that surrounds every human being. Each person's aura is different, like a thumbprint. It is sometimes described as looking like a bright, shifting ribbon of light encircling the individual's body, their personal *aurora borealis.*'"

"Make that *boring*-alis," Vinnie Carlucci cut in.

"I'll say," muttered Nick Carlucci. "So where's the info on making dough?"

Reaching across the table, I snatched my father's book out of Cleveland's grubby hands. "I can't believe you people!" I said, brushing the hair out of my face. "You think ESP is just some way of making money? Well, for your information, not

63

just anyone can read a book and suddenly have psychic powers. You have to believe in it and respect it. You have to be special!"

"Well, excuse us, Ms. Special," snapped Byron Prendergast.

"Yeah," Vinnie Carlucci said. "Sorry for stepping on your psychic toes."

"Hey, don't apologize to her," said Nick Carlucci. "As far as I'm concerned, she's not even psychic. She probably just got lucky."

"You're right," said Leonard Dooley. "All she did was guess one lousy test. That hardly qualifies as ESP."

"And so what if she has a smelly old book?" Cleveland added. "She also brought an umbrella to school this morning."

"Yeah," Byron snickered. "Like *that* makes sense."

As a matter of fact, it did.

At exactly three o'clock that afternoon, just as school was letting out—

C-c-c-crrraaaaackkk-booooom!

The sky was rocked by a giant clap of thunder.

Instantly, giant hailstones started raining down from above. White chunks of ice, some as big as

64

Ping-Pong balls, furiously pelted the street and sidewalk, and the line of yellow buses waiting at the curb.

Students who had been heading toward their rides started running in all directions, bumping into each other in the confusion.

In the teachers' parking lot, dozens of car alarms were triggered all at once, adding to the sense of chaos.

"Hit the decks!" hollered Byron Prendergast.

"What's happening?" cried Monica Myers, as the icy hail pelted her big hair.

"It's an alien attack!" shouted Cleveland Coopersmith, as hailstones ricocheted off the brim of his fedora.

Everyone was yelling and screaming.

Everyone except me.

Standing right in the middle of the running, stampeding throng, I calmly opened my umbrella, raised it high above my head, and then strode slowly and purposefully toward my bus.

Chapter 7

Ping!—Pffft!—Pong!—Ping!—Pffft!

The hailstones bounced off the roof of the bus as the doors hissed shut, the engine revved, and we left the school grounds.

"It's like a meteor shower," Cleveland Coopersmith said from the back of the bus, pushing his fedora hat back on his head and leaning close to the windows.

"What an ignorant remark," Gary Beck replied. "If this was a meteor shower, Cleveland, there would be nothing left of the bus. The strength and kinetic velocity would cause immense damage to the vehicle's fuselage."

"Oh shut up, Geck!" Cleveland sometimes liked to switch the letters of people's first and last names to irritate them.

I leaned against the window and looked up at the sky.

Then, just as suddenly as the hail had started, it stopped. It didn't even trickle to a halt, but just gave up all at once.

Weird.

The rest of the bus ride was pretty quiet. Everyone was more than a little freaked out by the sudden storm. Especially me.

I kept staring at the umbrella in my hands. Somehow, deep down, I had known something like this would happen. But how?

"He could always tell when a storm was coming. . . ."

Grandma Luisa's words rang in my ears.

I reached into my backpack and withdrew my father's book.

Not knowing what I was looking for, but sensing that the answer was somewhere inside, I opened the book to a random page and began to read.

Astral Projection

One of the most advanced psychic abilities, astral projection can be performed by only the most gifted clairvoyant. During astral projection, a psychic is able to leave his or her physical body behind, in a state of suspended animation, and travel freely through the psychic realm as a spirit. While astrally projecting, the individual exists as a being of pure energy—as his or her "life force," or spirit.

A note of warning: The following exercise is not to be attempted lightly. If a person's body is left unattended for too long, his or her spirit may not be able to reenter it. Before attempting to astrally project, novices should <u>seek the guidance of an experienced psychic.</u>

The last part of that paragraph had been underlined by my father.

Now the words seemed to jump up at me. It was as if my father had somehow known I would be reading this book, this particular passage, at this particular moment.

"Seek the guidance of an experienced psychic. . . ."

Of course.

Suddenly I knew where I could get the answers I was looking for.

Looking out the bus window, I saw we were on Central Avenue. I turned my head and watched the Metier Mall recede into the background.

The first stop was only a couple blocks from

the mall and I got off there. It wouldn't be a long walk back.

As soon as my feet hit the pavement, a strange sense of foreboding overcame me. Something wasn't quite right.

I looked up at the sky.

Aside from a chill in the air, there was no sign of further hailstorms. Everything was perfectly calm.

So why the strange feeling?

I took a deep breath and watched the cloud of cold form as I exhaled.

Okay, Elena, focus on what you have to do!

There it was—up ahead. The flashing neon palm and eyeball. It seemed to beckon me.

Rushing to the entrance, I reached for the door, pulled it open, and—

"Oh! Excuse me."

—collided with a tall woman, dressed in a long beige coat. She wore a plain scarf tied over her head. I recognized her almost immediately. She had auburn hair, blue eyes, and the same sharp features as her missing son, Todd.

"Mrs. Aldridge?" I said.

Todd Aldridge was a kid at my school. Last summer, he vanished without a trace. At first everyone thought he'd been kidnapped, because his family is really rich. But when no ransom note ever came, people figured maybe he'd been killed or something. The police searched all through the woods around town. They even dragged the town reservoir. But no body turned up.

Then, back in October, this psycho attacked another kid in my school, Ethan Rogers. The police think the same guy might have attacked Todd. The good news is that Ethan wasn't hurt. The bad news is that the man who attacked him died of a heart attack before the police could find out if he had taken Todd, too.

The weird part is, nobody knows who the dead guy was. There were no records on him at all. The Aldridges even put out a reward for any information on the stranger. When no one came forth, Mrs. Aldridge went on TV to ask if anyone had any clue as to who the man was.

That was the last time I'd seen her, pleading on television for any word of her lost son.

Now she looked startled. She gazed down at me, distracted.

"I'm sorry," she said. "Do I know you?"

"I'm Elena Vargas," I replied. "I went to school with Todd."

For a second her face was a blank. Then she smiled.

"Oh, of course. Elena. How are you?"

"I'm fine," I replied.

Looking up at her, I was reminded that not long ago Carol Aldridge had been a very beautiful woman. But I suppose losing your only child can take its toll. Since Todd's disappearance, her face had acquired a pale, haunted look. Her makeup did little to hide the dark circles under her eyes, or mask the worry lines that creased her forehead.

And yet, right now she seemed strangely happy.

"I'm sorry I didn't recognize you," she told me. "I'm afraid my mind is in a bit of a whir. I just had the most extraordinary experience!"

"Did you see Madame Mysteria?" I asked her.

"I certainly did," Mrs. Aldridge said, her voice bubbling over with excitement. "And I only wish I had visited her sooner!"

Her enthusiasm was contagious. "Why?" I asked eagerly. "What did she tell you?"

"The best news." Mrs. Aldridge placed her hand on my shoulder. "Oh, Elena . . . Todd is alive!"

Before I could respond, she continued in a rush of words:

"I know how it must sound," she said. "And believe me, before today I never believed in all this psychic mumbo jumbo. But you should have seen her, Elena! There are no tricks up this woman's sleeve. All she asked was to see a personal item of Todd's. I showed her his camera. It was his prized possession—a gift on his thirteenth birthday."

"Really?" I said.

"Madame Mysteria was able to tell me the most amazing things, just by holding it. She said it held a powerful energy. She could tell that Todd was alive and that he wants to come home, but that he can't find his way."

"He needs your help . . . ," I added.

I was getting a weird sense of déjà vu.

"Exactly! But that's not the best part." Mrs. Aldridge opened her purse and pulled out—

No, it can't be!

But there it was. A cylinder of black wax, about as thick around as my wrist.

My heart lodged in my throat.

It was the exact same kind of candle as Madame Mysteria had given to me! The one she had told me was "one of a kind"!

A bitter taste filled my mouth as Mrs. Aldridge recited familiar instructions. "Madame Mysteria says all I need to do is place this special candle in my window for seven nights in a row, and it will help guide Todd back to me."

Mrs. Aldridge didn't notice the look of shock on my face. She was too excited.

"Well, it was lovely running into you, Elena," she told me, tucking the candle back in her purse. "But I simply can't wait. I have to rush home and light this right away." Her voice was filled with giddy anticipation. "Just think . . . my Toddy is alive!"

I stood there frozen as Mrs. Aldridge waved her good-bye. Listening to the click of her heels recede in the distance, I could feel my heartbeat begin to race, my cheeks starting to burn.

Gritting my teeth, I pushed open the door and stormed into Madame Mysteria's waiting room.

Everything looked exactly as it had during my first visit. The magazines on the table lay spread out in a perfect fan, reflecting the glow from the lights blinking in the window. With every pink-and-yellow pulse, I could feel my temperature rise.

"Hello?" I called out, my fists balled in anger.

"Just a minute," Madame Mysteria's cheerful

voice called out from the back room. I heard footsteps. Then the velvet curtain parted and she emerged. "Welcome to Madame Mysteria's Psychic Parlor."

"Don't you mean 'Ruth Bogg's House of Deception'?" I snapped at her. My mouth was dry with rage.

When she saw who it was, the shock on her face was quickly replaced with a look of confusion.

"Why, Elena, I didn't expect to see you."

"I bet you didn't, you faker!" I said, my voice rising. "I came here to ask you some serious questions about psychic stuff that's been troubling me—and what do I discover?" I continued, not for a moment thinking she was going to answer. "I find you telling even *more* lies! Lies just like the ones you told *me!*"

Madame Mysteria's—or should I say, Ruth Bogg's—pale eyes flashed with concern.

"I never told you lies, Elena."

"Oh yes, you did!" I shouted. "I saw that candle you sold Mrs. Aldridge! You told me it was one of a kind! Is that how you make your money? Giving fake advice and phony candles to poor unsuspecting believers? How can you cheat people like that?"

I could feel my heart racing in my chest with every word that passed my lips.

"I don't cheat them," Madame Mysteria replied evenly. "I give them hope, Elena. I gave you hope about your father. Poor Mrs. Aldridge is in a great deal of pain and anguish about her son, Todd. Today, I gave her some peace of mind. If helping people is wrong, then perhaps I'm guilty of that. But I don't think so, Elena. I think what I'm doing is good."

"Good?" I shrieked at her. "Good to give *false* hope? To make me think there's actually something to look forward to when there isn't?"

How dare she mention my father? How dare she insult his memory like that?

I noticed that Madame Mysteria was holding a camera in her hands. Todd's camera. I reached over and snatched it out of her grasp.

"You have no right to hold onto this, Ms. Bogg! Keeping this is as good as stealing it from that woman! I'm going to give it back!"

"Elena, please stop this."

"You know what you are? You're not Madame Mysteria! You're not a psychic or anything like that! My grandmother has a name for people like you, Ruth Bogg. You're *una mentirosa!* You know what that means? It means you're a liar!"

I turned on my heels and marched out of Madame Mysteria's phony psychic shop, Todd Aldridge's camera clutched tightly in my hand.

Ruth's voice called after me, but I ignored her and kept going.

The only thing that was important was to return the camera to Mrs. Aldridge as soon as possible and explain to her what had happened. I felt just awful for poor Carol Aldridge. She was going to be terribly disappointed to learn that she had been deceived.

But it's better to know the truth, I thought.

It's better to see things clearly than to look at the world through lies.

Chapter 8

A sharp, biting wind was blowing when I stepped out into the parking lot, leaving the mall.

I searched the rows of snow-covered cars, looking for Mrs. Aldridge's dark blue Volvo. I knew the car well from all the times I had seen Todd step out of it, back before August, before he disappeared off the face of the earth.

"Mrs. Aldridge!" I yelled into the cold winter air. My voice seemed louder and crisper because of the cold. Winter always made sounds seem sharper than usual.

But no one answered.

"Mrs. Aldridge!" I called again.

Then I saw it. The Aldridges' dark blue Volvo

was pulling out of its parking space on the far side of the lot.

I had only one choice.

Holding the camera firmly in my hands so as not to drop it, I began running in the direction of the car.

"Wait! Wait, Mrs. Aldridge! Don't go!" I shouted.

But my cries were in vain.

Mrs. Aldridge couldn't hear me.

The car backed out of its space, crunching the snow beneath its tires. Its tailpipe coughed small clouds of exhaust fumes into the air.

Just as I reached the space where it had been parked, the car left the lot and turned right on Central Avenue.

I heaved a deep sigh of frustration and watched Mrs. Aldridge disappear into the grayness of the late afternoon.

They've all been lies. Every one of them. The candle is a fake, my so-called visions were fakes, and my father really is dead.

I didn't want to cry. I didn't want to think about any of it. I didn't want to acknowledge the fact that the kids at school had been right.

I never predicted anything.

I don't have any psychic powers.

I'm as big a fake as Madame Mysteria!

This last thought was just too much to consider.

I looked down at the camera I held in my hands. Todd's camera.

Now, I don't know much about cameras, but I know enough to recognize an expensive model when I see it. This was a fancy camera, all right.

I thought about Todd. About how his hands had once held this camera, too.

Then something very strange happened.

A weird sensation overcame me, standing there in the mall's parking lot.

It was as if my feet were leaving the ground. I suddenly felt very light and airy.

Looking down at my feet, I saw that they were firmly on the ground. Several inches of snow covered my shoes.

But still the feeling kept coming over me in waves.

Suddenly, a searing hot surge pulsated up my arms into my spine and caused me to lose my breath for a second.

It was coming from the camera!

Without thinking, I slowly raised the camera to my face and looked through the viewfinder.

I blinked and swallowed hard at what I saw.

Trees!

I saw trees!

Well, that's not so strange, I thought.

But then I lowered the camera and looked in the direction I had been pointing it.

I had pointed it right at one of the parked cars.

Looking through the viewfinder again, I was amazed to see trees where the car was supposed to be.

What's going on?

The light-headed feeling I had intensified. I felt dizzy, as though I were about to lose my balance and fall over.

But I was standing perfectly still.

My hands trembling, I once more raised the camera and looked.

In the flash of an eye, I thought I had been hit by lightning. It all came to me so fast, I could barely make sense of it all.

In the viewfinder, I saw more trees, dozens and dozens of them, streaming past like when you look at them from the window of a speeding car.

And a fence. A tall chain-link fence rattling in the wind.

The fence had a sign on it. I couldn't quite make it out. It was all so hazy.

And then water. A lake of some kind.

No, not a lake.

I lowered the camera slowly. I recognized the place I'd just seen.

The town reservoir.

I was convinced that what I'd just seen had been a genuine, true-to-life psychic vision.

There was no other way to explain it. What was the word in my father's book?

I had experienced "psychometry" through Todd Aldridge's camera!

But now what?

I looked across the parking lot, toward a high chain-link fence with woods on the other side. The reservoir was through those woods.

I considered going to the reservoir. I could sense within me something telling me to go there. True, it was getting late, but the feeling was powerful.

That's when I realized that I had already begun to walk in the direction of the woods.

Without knowing it, my feet had taken over

and I was trudging through the snow of the parking lot, heading for the high chain-link fence that surrounded the watershed area.

I have to go there, I reasoned to myself.

Obviously, there was some kind of psychic connection between Todd Aldridge and me. It was as though he were trying to communicate with me through his camera, as if he were trying to tell me something. It was my obligation—my duty—to find out what it was.

Then I can tell Mrs. Aldridge the truth!

A smile cracked its way across my lips as I thought of bringing Carol Aldridge some real information about her son. Not a lie, like Madame Mysteria had given her.

As I left the parking lot, walking became harder and slower because of a thick blanket of snow on the ground.

A cold wind whipped through the trees in the distance up ahead, swaying the naked branches on the other side of the fence, giving them an eerie, frightening look.

They look like skeletons, waiting for me!

I gulped and dismissed the thought. That time it wasn't a psychic vision. It was just my imagination working overtime.

I continued to walk through the snow.

Reaching the fence, I realized I would have to climb over it. I knew there was a hole in the fence somewhere that some eighth-graders had made, but I couldn't remember where it was.

It would be too difficult to climb the fence with all the things I was carrying. I took off my backpack and laid it in the snow at the foot of the fence with my umbrella. I figured it would be safe to leave my stuff there. It was pretty well concealed.

Climbing up was tricky even without the extra baggage. Getting my feet into the diamond-shaped holes and balancing myself and the camera as the wind blew—well, it was no picnic. Getting down was easier.

Luckily, a large snowdrift rested against the other side of the fence and I jumped into it. The soft snow cushioned my fall.

I stood up, brushed myself off, and headed for the woods.

Spotting a path, I decided to take it.

It must lead to the reservoir, I figured.

As I walked down the path, I began to think about Todd Aldridge. Every time I blinked my eyes, his face somehow appeared to me in my mind's eye. His dark hair, his blue eyes, his mischievous smile . . .

I started to wonder if Todd had ever walked down this path. Then, somehow—I can't explain how exactly—I knew he had. I could feel it.

The light-headed warm glow I had felt in the mall's parking lot returned and I could sense that Todd Aldridge had taken this very same route.

A strange tickling sensation in my stomach told me that when Todd had walked down the path, something had not been right about it.

Suddenly, my feet stopped in their tracks without my willing it.

Another shocking bolt of heat rushed through me, this time starting at my toes and working its way up to my head.

I knew what it was.

When Todd Aldridge had walked here, he had been in extreme danger!

Looking around, I saw that I was surrounded by trees on all sides. Only the slim path wove through the angular branches.

For a moment, I worked on steadying my breath. I watched the white clouds that I blew from my mouth return to an even puff.

I lifted the camera to my face and looked through the viewfinder.

What? But how?

I was looking at the same exact trees as those that stood around me. But through the viewfinder, the trees were lush and green and covered in leaves.

In the camera's eye, no snow lay on the ground. A warm, gentle breeze whistled through the swaying branches.

A bolt shot through me, this time almost knocking me off my feet, and I knew exactly what I was seeing.

I was seeing the woods as they appeared last August. I was seeing the trees as they were on the very day Todd Aldridge had disappeared!

I was looking into the past!

For a moment, I closed my eyes.

The cold breeze turned warm against my cheek and I could feel the sun shining down on me. My nostrils filled with the rich aromas of summer.

From where I stood with my eyes firmly shut, I could hear bees buzzing in the flowers and the gentle rustle of the leaves above. Grass seemed to sway at my feet and the August sun beat down on the top of my head.

Opening my eyes, I discovered myself right back where I had been. Snow covered my feet, the trees were bare and still, and the flowers were dead, their roots asleep deep beneath the ground. A cold wind made my teeth chatter.

I looked through the camera again and saw summer once more.

Slowly, carefully, I began to walk, still looking through the viewfinder.

As I walked, the forest in all its green richness opened before me.

A bird flew by, chirping, weaving its way through the branches of a tall tree.

But then something began to feel very wrong. Very wrong indeed.

I had the sensation that someone—or something—was watching me from deep within the woods. Something evil. Something that wished me harm.

I've got to get away.

The thought flashed through my mind. I didn't know if it had been Todd's thought, or mine.

But the fear in my gut was definitely my own.

I lowered the camera—

And felt a hand grab me sharply from behind.

Chapter 9

I whirled around, screaming, expecting to see something horrible.

Instead, I saw three kids standing in front of me.

Ethan Rogers, Ashley Rose, and Jack Raynes. Fellow seventh-graders.

"Don't be frightened," Jack said, removing his hand from my shoulder. "It's only us."

"*Now* you tell me?" I croaked, my heart still pounding in panic mode in my chest. "You know, you could've said something before jumping out and grabbing me like that."

"We did call to you," Ashley said. "But you didn't hear us."

"Yeah . . . you looked like you were in some

kind of trance or something," Ethan confirmed.

"What are you doing out here?" Jack asked me.

I wasn't sure I should tell them the truth. Start telling people you're following the "psychometric trail" of a missing kid and they'll probably think you're nuts.

"Oh . . . I'm just taking some photographs," I lied, holding up Todd's camera as evidence.

"With the lens cap on?" said Ethan. He reached over and plucked a black plastic disk off the front of Todd's camera.

"Oops." I chuckled nervously and decided to change the subject. "So . . . what are *you* guys doing here?" I asked.

"Following you," the three of them said in unison.

I blinked. It wasn't the answer I expected.

"Following me?" I said as they all started moving in closer to me. "Why?"

"Because you showed the signs," Jack answered.

"The signs? What are you talking about?"

"Well, it's your thirteenth birthday, for starters," said Ethan.

"And suddenly you're claiming you're psychic," added Ashley.

90

"And then there's *this.*"

Before I knew what was happening, Jack reached out, seized hold of my hand, and jabbed the point of something sharp—a pin?—into the tip of my index finger.

"Hey!" I cried, yanking my hand away and bringing my smarting finger to my mouth. "What did you do that for?"

"Because," Ashley answered, "we need to see your blood."

See my blood? I thought.

"Why?" I asked, sucking on my tiny wound.

"To check out what color it is," Ethan said matter-of-factly.

And to think I'd *been worried about sounding nuts.*

For a minute I just stared at the three of them, shifting my gaze from one face to the next.

They each looked dead serious.

"Okayyyyy," I replied, deciding it would be best to humor them. I withdrew the finger from my mouth and held it up for them to see. "See?" I said. "Red, just like yours."

The three kids glanced at my finger. Then they all shared a look.

"Well, you're right about one thing," said Jack.

"It *is* just like ours," Ethan continued.

"But it isn't red," Ashley finished.

"What are you talking ab—" I began, only to hear the words disappear as all the air instantly drained from my lungs.

A perfectly round drop of blood was beading on the tip of my finger. And it wasn't red.

It was *silver*.

I stared, speechless, as the drop grew bigger. My hand started shaking. My brain could barely function. I had to concentrate to make words form.

"B-b-but . . . this can't be. My blood is *red*," I insisted as the sticky metallic liquid dribbled down my finger like a stream of mercury. "At least . . . it used to be."

"*Used* to be," said Ethan. "Ours too. Until our thirteenth birthdays. That's when it happens."

"When *what* happens?"

"It starts out feeling like a cold," Jack said. "You get headaches, and dizzy spells, and your senses start going out of whack—"

"And then you get your powers," said Ashley.

My mind was spinning. I tried to make sense of what they were all saying.

"You mean . . . you guys are psychic, too?"

Ashley shook her head. "So far it's been different

for each one of us." She frowned. "That's the weird part."

"*That's* the weird part?" I squeaked. "What's the *normal* part?"

She ignored my remark. "When I turned thirteen I got these amazing aquatic abilities. Suddenly I could swim faster and farther than ever before. I can stay underwater for hours on end, even in freezing temperatures. My hearing is supersensitive, like a dolphin's. If I'm injured, I can even regenerate parts of myself, like a frog."

"Ribbit, ribbit," Jack Raynes cracked. Ashley glared at him.

"And what can you do, Jack?" I asked him.

The red-headed boy looked at me. "Do you remember how I started speaking Spanish so well last November?"

I nodded. How could I forget? After he had made Mrs. Martinez look stupid in front of her whole Spanish class, it was all anybody had talked about.

"Well, it turns out I can speak *any* language," Jack continued. "It's like I have a translating microchip in my brain. I can understand most all forms of verbal or written communication, including computer codes and insect language. I can even send my own faxes—check this out."

Jack opened his mouth and emitted a high-pitched staticky tweedle. It sounded just like a computer modem, only way louder. It made me wince.

"Show-off," Ashley said, sticking her fingers in her ears.

Jack stopped making the fax noise and grinned at her.

It was Ethan's turn. "I've become a fighting machine," he said, hiking his Wolverine backpack up on his shoulder. "It's like my brain has been programmed with all sorts of martial arts moves. I know how to use any weapon—instinctively. I have lightning-quick reflexes, heat-sensing vision that lets me see in the dark, and a venomous bite . . . like a snake."

My mouth was hanging open in disbelief.

Snake venom? Insect language? Dolphin hearing?

Ashley noticed my shocked expression.

"I know it's a bit much to deal with, Elena. But you have to face it. You're one of us. You've changed."

"But why?" I said. "Why me? Why us?"

"What do you know about your father?" Ethan asked.

The question threw me. "Well, he—"

"—disappeared when you were four years old," Jack cut in.

I nodded.

"And didn't have any close relatives—aside from your mom and you," Ashley said.

I nodded again. "How do you know all that?"

"Because we've compared notes," Ethan said. "It turns out, aside from silver blood, each of us has at least one parent who disappeared nine years ago."

"The question is," Jack said, "did they really disappear . . . or did they *go back?*"

"Go back?" I said. "To where?"

Jack raised a finger toward the sky.

I heard myself laugh. "You think our parents are *aliens?*" I asked. "That's crazy!"

"As crazy as silver blood?" Ashley cut in.

"Or being able to tell the future?" Jack added.

I stopped laughing. They had a point.

"There's a reason so many people say they've seen UFOs around town," said Ethan. "It's because they *have.*"

I thought about my father. About my vision of him, heading into the spaceship. About how little I truly knew about him.

And about how much I wanted answers.

I looked at the three kids standing before me.

"Tell me everything you know," I said.

"We will," said Ethan. "But not here. It's too dangerous. Follow us."

Ethan, Ashley, and Jack led the way through the woods. They moved swiftly and surely along the snow-covered trail. It was hard for me to keep up.

I also felt that I was being left behind mentally. My brain tried to grapple with the extraordinary information it was being told.

I kept looking at my index finger, even though it had stopped bleeding minutes ago.

"You're saying our parents were aliens that landed in Metier, married humans, had us kids, and then decided to take off when we were four?"

The others nodded.

"But I don't think they wanted to leave," Ashley said quietly. "I think they were forced to. Someone came for them."

"Someone . . . or some*thing*," said Jack.

The way he said "something" gave me goose bumps.

"What are you talking about?"

The others shared another look.

"We have to tell her," Ethan said. Jack and Ashley nodded solemnly.

"Yeah, tell me," I said, scurrying to catch up

with them. "I mean, it can't be any worse than the silver blood part, right?" I laughed nervously.

I was met with stony silence.

"Just a little," Ethan said.

"You see," Jack explained, "we don't just get powers on our thirteenth birthday. We get company."

Ashley shot the boys a look. "What those two are trying to say is that something has come after each of us. An alien creature that tried to kill us around our thirteenth birthday."

"Each of us managed to escape, but it always comes back," said Ethan.

I waited for someone to elaborate, but the other kids were strangely quiet. They each seemed to be lost in some dark, private memory.

Jack was the first to snap out of it. "Look," he said to me, pointing into the distance.

Up ahead, jutting above the treetops, I could just make out a tall skeletal structure glinting in the long rays of the setting sun. It looked like a smaller, skinnier version of the Eiffel Tower.

"What is it?" I asked.

"That's where we're headed," said Ethan. "It's Ed Beister's radio antenna."

"Ed Beister?" I said. "Mister Transistor? The town's tinfoil quack?"

"Turns out old man Beister is not as wacko as he seems," said Ashley.

"He's the only other person who knows about us," said Jack. "He's been using his radio tower to monitor alien radio transmissions for years."

"In fact," Ashley added, "it was Ed who first noticed that there'd been a UFO sighting and transmission on each of our thirteenth birthdays."

"If our guess is correct," said Ethan, "we should be receiving some transmissions any second now—because it's *your* birthday." He nodded at me.

We had come upon a thick stand of evergreen trees, growing so close together that they looked like a dark green, furry wall. Ethan was already pushing his way between the snowy boughs of two trees. Soon he disappeared from view. Ashley followed close behind.

"Ed's radio tower is just through here," Jack explained, turning sideways. "It's a bit of a squeeze, but not too bad." The tree branches bent as he pushed through them, then whipped back into place, sending snow cascading to the ground. "Just keep your mouth closed, or you'll be eating pine needles." Then the boughs closed over him, and he was gone.

I was about to follow, when I was filled with

the same sickening dizzy sensation that I'd been getting all day. My head throbbed—

And it was like a flashbulb going off in my brain.

I suddenly had a vision of Ethan, Jack, and Ashley: The three of them were standing in the snow, staring at something at their feet. Their eyes were different somehow . . . harder, colder. I followed their downward gaze and saw what they were looking at.

Ice water ran through my veins.

They were looking at a body.

Lying motionless on its back on the forest floor.

My body.

As abruptly as it came, the vision vanished.

I was staring at the branches of the evergreen trees. Watching as they swayed from where the other kids had just pushed through.

They're going to kill me, I thought. *Right now they're on the other side of these trees, waiting for me to emerge, planning their attack.*

"Elena?" called Ashley from the other side of the trees. "Are you okay?"

"I'm fine," I called back, trying to keep my voice as normal as possible. "Just tying my shoe. I'll be there in a minute."

Instead, I turned and ran.

_____ Chapter 10

And I kept running.

Low-hanging branches grabbed at my hair and swiped at my arms and legs, but I didn't stop. I shielded my face with the back of my arms and continued to run, my heart pounding in fear, my legs churning up snow.

My foot hit a jutting tree root. I fell forward, landing on my knees, bracing myself with the palms of my hands. I felt the icy coldness of the ground and pushed myself up.

And kept running.

My breath came in short, shallow gasps as my feet plowed onward through the snow and fallen branches.

My legs were aching from the cold and from the fall I had taken, but still I ran.

No! No! No! It can't be!

The image of my face lying there on the ground—dead—haunted me. With every blink of my eyes, there it was again.

Tears began to blur my vision and push their way down my cheeks.

It can't be true! It isn't true! Oh, please, please, please make it not be true!

Suddenly, the trees gave way and I found myself standing before a tall chain-link fence.

I stopped, and bending over with my hands on my knees, tried to catch my breath. I shot a quick look over my shoulder to see if I had been followed.

No. I was alone.

The fence gleamed in the dying rays of sunlight. I realized where I had come.

I was right back where I started.

In the distance, the mall looked sad and uninhabited. A chill breeze whistled across the nearly deserted parking lot.

With a pang of remorse, I realized that I no longer had Todd Aldridge's camera with me. I must have dropped it when I fell.

So, you lost his camera, I told myself. *At least you saved your life.*

But had I really?

What did Jack, Ashley, and Ethan want from me? I wondered. *Were they out to kill me?*

I didn't know what to believe anymore, but I knew one thing for certain.

I needed to stay as far away from Jack and Ashley and Ethan as I could.

If what I saw was really a premonition of my own death, and they were somehow involved, the only sane thing to do would be to keep my distance.

Drying my tears and checking myself for bruises or scratches, I prepared to climb back over the fence and leave the reservoir area.

But then I heard it.

A sound from within the woods.

A loud, low-pitched humming, echoing through the air.

For the briefest second, I thought it was Jack or Ethan coming to get me. But then I realized that the sound wasn't human.

It was the sound of some kind of machine.

The hum began to grow louder as I tried to peer through the overhanging branches to see its source. It seemed to be coming nearer.

Then something caught my eye.

High above the trees, in the clouds above the reservoir, a mysterious blue light began to flash. With every hum, the light pulsed brighter.

I watched as slowly the clouds began to move and twist and turn. The light breeze that had been blowing grew in strength until it started to gust.

Before my very eyes, I saw the cloud cover change shape. It formed into a long, tall funnel shape—like a tornado, only upside-down. It was like staring up into a bottomless whirlpool of clouds.

I grabbed hold of the fence, suddenly afraid that I might be sucked up into the swirling, pulsating sky.

Then my eyes opened wide and my jaw dropped in disbelief.

There, from the center of the cloud funnel, appeared a large round object, glinting with blue lights.

It was a UFO!

The circular craft descended through the funnel of clouds, and for a brief moment hung in the air, hovering.

Slowly, six spindly legs unfolded from the lower half of the metal sphere. Once they had locked into place, it began to land somewhere on the other side of the trees standing before me.

Without thinking, I began pushing my way toward it.

The branches parted with a shove of my arm and I proceeded back into the woods, following the glowing blue lights that shined from beyond.

As I neared the edge of the reservoir, the lights grew brighter and stronger. Emerging from the woods and reaching the water's edge, I saw the flying saucer in full view.

The glowing metal sphere was about twenty feet in diameter. Its legs held it about ten feet above the frozen shore. Its lights pulsed bright blue.

The hum was louder than ever.

I shielded my eyes from the glare and could just make out some kind of central hatch on the underside of the craft as it opened. An even brighter light shone out from within.

It was just like in my dream!

My heart skipped a beat as one thought and one thought only screamed its way through my brain. . . .

Dad!

Suddenly, I knew my father was inside that spaceship. I can't explain the clarity of that thought, but it came to me with such a jolt, I simply knew it had to be true.

All I wanted to do was go to him, see him, talk to him. I had to tell him how much I missed him.

I had to ask him about my psychic powers. About my silver blood. He would know. He would understand and make everything better. I had to feel the bear hug he used to give me when I was a toddler. The one that made me feel safe and secure no matter what.

My feet led the way and I followed.

Slowly approaching the spacecraft, I squinted in the shining blue light.

As I drew nearer, it was as if the huge metal structure could read my mind. A long ramp descended from the hatchway and touched the ground.

It has to be my dad doing this! I thought. *He wants to see me! I just know it!*

I mounted the ramp, and shielding my face from the glare, climbed inside the craft.

It took a moment for my vision to adjust. Then, blinking rapidly, I looked around. Icy fingers danced down my spine.

It was exactly like my dream in every detail!

Computers lined the walls of the spacecraft. Their monitors blinked with strange colors and readouts. Buttons flashed and winked. The cool metal surface of the floor was smooth and slick, with an almost transparent quality.

And there, standing in the middle of the control

room, was a figure with his back turned. I could almost have cried from excitement.

It was him! It was my dad!

Trying to speak, I found my mouth was dry and my voice cracked. I tried again.

"Dad?"

But he couldn't hear me over the loud humming of the craft. He remained staring at one of the computer monitors.

I stepped up to him and gently placed my hand on his shoulder.

"Oh, Dad, it's really you!" I said.

"Guess again," hissed an inhuman, horrible voice.

Chapter 11

The man turned around slowly.

I realized I had made a terrible mistake.

His features did look like my father's, but horribly distorted, like a Halloween mask on a shelf. The skin was pale and hung slack on his face.

The worst part was his eyes.

They were two flat, soulless circles sunken deep in his dead flesh, two panes of black glass with no life behind them. I stared into their depths, too astonished to scream.

Panic only hit when I felt him grab me, hard and swift. His cold reptilian skin was like a vise around my wrists. I screamed and jerked, my hair falling over my face as I struggled.

It was no use.

His hands were like two bands of iron. I felt a stab of pain as he tightened his grip, and in an instant I was on my knees.

I knew he could break my wrists if he chose to.

"Who are you?" I cried out. "What have you done with my father?"

The alien laughed softly to itself, enjoying my distress. Then it jerked me to my feet. I bit my lip to hide the pain, unwilling to give it the satisfaction of seeing how much it hurt.

He reached over and pressed a flat, yellow square on the console in front of him. With a soft *whoosh*, a thick plastic tube shot down around my body, encasing me. My arms were pinned to my sides.

The alien lifted a small microphone from the console. He pressed it against the hollow of his throat. "I am here," he said. I saw that his lips barely moved, but his throat pulsed as he talked. I shuddered, thinking of that creature's hands on me. "I have her."

There was the static crackling of a distant radio transmission, then a reply through the console. "That is satisfactory," a voice said, just as creepy and inhuman as my captor's. "Is she alive?"

The alien swiveled its terrible blank stare in my direction. I was breathing heavily, fogging the yellowish plastic of the tube.

"For the moment," he said.

"That is satisfactory," the voice said again. "Have you acquired the other targets?"

"Not yet," he said. "The two boys and the other girl are still active."

The other targets—they were talking about Ethan, Jack, and Ashley! I realized, too late, how wrong I had been.

If only I had stuck with them—if only I hadn't run away! How could I have thought that they were a threat to my life? But the vision had been so real!

"You have sixty minutes to bring back the others," said the voice on the console. "Then your ship must return to the central base."

The alien clenched his fist. "I will not fail."

"Good," the voice said. "Failure will not be tolerated." The transmitter crackled again, then went dead.

"You'll never get them," I screamed. "They're too smart. They're ready for you."

The alien tapped numbers into a timer strapped to its wrist. Then it stared directly into my eyes. It laughed softly, a chilling noise.

"You're right," it said. "They are ready for me."

As he said the words, his body began shaking. His shoulders spasmed in bursts. I saw the skin on his face stretching and contorting, as if the bones were rearranging themselves underneath. The whole time, his eyes never left mine. I wanted to scream, but the tube was so tight that I could barely breathe.

Suddenly, the alien hunched over. Then his shaking subsided.

"They are ready for me," he repeated, slowly straightening up. "But they're not ready for *you*."

He looked straight into my eyes, smiling.

It was the coldest smile I've ever seen in my life. But that wasn't what terrified me. What terrified me was his face.

Because it was *my* face.

He had transformed himself into my twin.

The sight made me gag. Seeing my face with those hideous black eyes . . . I felt as if I'd been robbed. Violated.

As I watched, the creature's eyes started shrinking, becoming human-sized. The blackness constricted, getting smaller until it was just a tiny pinprick in each eye. For a second I was staring into two blank white eyeballs. Then the color filled in, like two brown ink stains.

The transformation was complete.

The others would have no idea that it wasn't me.

My impostor tapped numbers into a timer on its wrist. "Don't try anything foolish," it said. "I

112

will return for you when I have your friends."

I watched, helplessly, as my double left the space-craft. The red display on the timer read "59:00."

One hour. That was how much time I had left.

I squirmed in the tube, trying to free myself. My clothing was damp with perspiration. The plastic chafed against my skin. Other than rubbing myself raw, I wasn't getting anywhere.

I thought briefly about the keys in my pocket—Could I get at them and scratch through the plastic?—but quickly rejected the idea. I would be lucky to even get my hand into my pocket, let alone get anything out of it. The plastic looked very strong and was easily an inch thick. And if by some miracle I *could* scratch a hole, what then? I would still be just as trapped.

It was hopeless. There was no way my body was getting out of the tube.

That was when the idea came to me.

My *body* wasn't getting out, but what about my *spirit*?

What if I could "astrally project" my soul out of my body, like I'd read about in my father's book?

I clenched my eyes and went through the steps in my head. I stopped struggling against my confinement, forcing my muscles to relax. I breathed as shallowly as possible, concentrating my mind and my spiritual energies at the center of my being. With my eyes closed, I conjured up a picture of my body, trapped in the tube, and pushed away from it.

After a few minutes of concentration, I opened my eyes. *Nothing had happened.* I was still in the tube.

It was a stupid idea, anyway. Had I really thought it would work? I was angry with myself. I had wasted precious minutes on a foolish idea. My friends were going to die, and it was all my fault.

As I struggled to think of another plan, I ran my hand through my hair, something I often do when I get frustrated. That was when I realized: My hands were free! How was it possible? Suddenly, it dawned on me.

It had worked after all! I *was* out of my body. I was simply standing in the same place as it was.

Cautiously, I took my first baby step away from the tube.

Instantly, I felt myself falling. I flailed my arms in a helpless panic, trying to catch on to anything, but it did no good. My heart went to my mouth. It was like the steepest plunge on the tallest roller coaster in the entire world. What had I done?

Then, mercifully, my fall stopped.

I was floating.

I felt warm, weightless, like a soap bubble on a current of air. I almost laughed out loud. I could see my body behind me, stuck in the tube, looking peacefully asleep. I wanted to find a way to free myself, but there was no time for that. I had to warn the others.

I felt myself rising. Right toward the ceiling of the control room. I tensed, braced for the impact—

And then I was outside, looking down at the top of the UFO beneath me.

I had passed through the solid metal wall of the spaceship, as easily as breaking through the surface of a pool.

I could detect the faint smell of pine needles in the air of the woods, but I didn't feel the icy January wind. I felt warm, safe, and happy. *I'll have to try this again when I have more time*, I thought.

And I continued to rise. Up and up, like a helium balloon.

Soon I was soaring high above the trees like a bird. I had always wanted to be able to fly. This was a fantasy come true. For a second I wondered how high I could go—all the way into outer space?

But I didn't have time to find out.

I remembered the warning from the book: If you spent too long outside of your body, you'd never be able to get back in.

From my viewpoint high above the forest, it was easy to spot the thin needle of Ed Beister's "space antenna" glinting in the sun, and I followed it to the ground.

At its base, I saw Jack, Ethan, and Ashley, talking in worried tones about my disappearance.

At first I was surprised that they didn't look at me as I touched down. Then I remembered that they couldn't see me. "Hey, guys," I shouted. "I'm back!"

They still didn't look up. What was going on? Were they ignoring me on purpose, because I'd run away? "Guys, over here!" I said urgently. "I'm sorry about before, but this is important!"

When even that didn't get their attention, I realized what was going on.

Apparently, without my body, I couldn't make any noise!

I tried to pick up a fallen branch and watched my ghostlike fingers pass right through it. So I couldn't even write in the snow that covered the forest floor, or shake my friends to get their attention.

Had I really come this far, only to be totally unable to warn them? I was as frustrated as I'd ever been in my entire life.

Where's a Ouija board when you need one! I thought to myself.

As those words passed through my mind, Jack looked up. "What did you say?" he asked Ashley.

"I didn't say anything," she said. "Why?"

Before he could answer, a figure emerged from the mass of evergreens.

It was me—or at least it looked just like me.

I knew it was the alien, but how could I warn my friends?

"Elena!" Ethan said. "Where did you go? We were worried for you."

"That's not me!" I shouted. "Jack, Ashley, Ethan—listen to me!" But they didn't respond.

"I found something in the woods," the fake Elena said in a monotone. "I think you guys should take a look."

Ashley looked at Ethan, worried. "All right," Ethan said. "We're coming. Just don't run off again."

I was seething with frustration. I couldn't believe they were falling for this obvious impostor. *Do they really think I talk like that?* I thought.

Jack looked up again. He turned to Ashley. "Did you just say something?" he asked.

Ashley got mad. "Cut it out, Jack," she said. "This is no time to be kidding around."

"I'm not kidding," he said. "I heard something. A girl's voice."

He heard me! He heard my thoughts! I screwed up my telepathic power and concentrated on Jack. *Stop!* I silently screamed. *Don't go with her! She's an impostor!*

Jack looked from side to side, clearly wondering if he was going crazy. Then he looked "Elena" in the eyes. "I don't want to be difficult or anything," he said, stopping in his tracks. "But where exactly are you taking us?"

"The reservoir," the fake Elena said. "You have to see what's there."

"Why don't you just tell us what it is and save us the trip?" Jack said reasonably.

"Jack, come on," said Ethan. "We've got to trust each other."

Jack took a deep breath. "I trust you and Ashley," he said. "And I trust Elena. But this isn't Elena."

My impostor smiled innocently. "You guys," she started, looking from one to the other. "You just had to make this difficult, didn't you?"

"Uh-oh," Ashley said as "Elena's" eyes expanded into large black holes.

Letting out a ghastly, inhuman howl, the alien charged at them.

_____ Chapter 12

But before it got any further, its body jerked, and it did a nosedive into the snow of the forest floor.

Behind it stood an old man with bushy gray hair and a beard, looking sort of like Santa in a tinfoil suit. He held a thick baseball bat–sized branch clenched in his fist.

"Hi," Ed Beister said, grinning from ear to ear. "I thought you kids could use some help."

Ethan bent over the body. Jack and Ashley crowded in closely to get a better look. I realized that this was the vision I'd had: the three of them surrounding my fallen body. As we watched, it transformed into the thin, sinister-looking creature I'd seen in the spacecraft.

"Ethan, don't touch him," Ashley said.

"He looks dead," Jack said.

"Haven't you seen any horror movies? They *always* look dead."

Ethan pressed two fingers to the alien's throat. "Well, I don't know too much about extraterrestrial anatomy," he said, "but I don't think his heart's beating."

The four of them let out a collective sigh of relief.

"Jack, how did you know she was an impostor?" Ashley asked. "What tipped you off?"

"Elena told me," he said. "I heard her inside my head. I don't know how, but somehow she's here, with us."

Hi guys, I transmitted silently through my thoughts. *Qué pasa?*

They laughed out loud. "I told you she was okay!" Ethan said.

Actually, I told them, *I'm not. I'm astrally projecting right now—but my body is still trapped in the alien spaceship. And if I stay out here much longer, I'll never be able to get my spirit back into my skin.*

"We'll take care of you," Jack said. "Just show us where the ship is, and we'll get you out."

Okay, I thought. *Just hurry.*

*　　　*　　　*

Ethan stayed behind with Ed to watch the alien body. I led Jack and Ashley through the woods as quickly as I could. Guiding someone on foot as a spirit traveling without a body proved to be harder than I expected. I couldn't show them the way. I could only transmit the occasional *left, right,* or *straight ahead.* And I'd never walked the path myself, only floated above it, so I wasn't sure exactly where we were going.

To make matters worse, after a few minutes my mind started to drift. I was losing my ability to concentrate.

Suddenly, going back into my body didn't seem like such a good idea. Why go back to feeling cold and wet when it snowed, to feeling hungry, or angry, or sad? I could stay like this forever, warm and peaceful. Maybe I wouldn't go back after all.

Then suddenly I was overcome by a weird prickly sensation.

And I had another thought flash.

There was the alien, on the ground where we'd left him. But instead of lying still, he was sitting up. And he had his hands wrapped around Ed Beister's throat.

I remembered the incredible strength of the alien's grip on my wrist.

He would kill the old man in a matter of seconds!

The vision passed as suddenly as it came. I knew it was a premonition. It would come true—if it hadn't already.

It's Mr. Beister, I thought to Jack. *He's in trouble!*

"What's wrong?" Jack asked.

That alien isn't dead, I answered. *I have to go back and warn Mr. Beister and Ethan, or they'll be killed.*

"But you can't go back," Ashley protested. "You don't have any time. You said so yourself. If you spend too long out of your body, you can never go back in again."

"I'll go instead," Jack said. "Ashley can get you out of that spacecraft."

No, I transmitted. *You'll never make it in time on foot. I have to do this myself. Mr. Beister saved our lives. Now I have to save his.*

Jack was about to say something else, but I was already gone.

I never moved so fast before in my entire life.

Leaves, branches, and startled forest animals flew past me in a blur. In an instant, I was back where we'd just been, at Ed Beister's space antenna.

There was Ed, bending over the alien to get a

122

closer look. I was just in time. Ed was saying something to Ethan—"I thought I saw it move"—but his voice sounded far-off and distant.

I was beginning to fade again.

Suddenly, all this seemed pointless. I was just going to drift away, just float, just be at peace. . . .

No sooner had I thought the words than I saw the alien's hand shoot up and grab Ed by the throat, just as he had in the vision. I had failed! The old man clawed at the hand desperately, but he was no match for the alien's strength. Ed slowly went limp, struggling more and more feebly until he went as limp as a rag doll.

I screamed out loud. I screamed a scream that no one could hear.

The alien tossed Ed's unconscious body to one side and stood up, facing Ethan. Ethan looked at the woods behind him. The trees were so close together, he'd never be able to run away fast enough. He was trapped. His only chance was to fight.

With a speed that I'd never seen before, Ethan ducked as the creature lunged for him, stepping under the blow. Then Ethan used the creature's own weight against it, judo style, to hurl it to the ground.

Unfazed, the alien rolled and landed on its feet in a crouch, like an attacking panther. He squared off with the thirteen-year-old boy, snarling and shaking in anger. I saw Ethan's eyes narrow. He looked ready for a fight.

Again, the creature charged, and this time Ethan sidestepped, hitting the alien with a flurry of kicks and punches as it passed him. The alien turned with a sudden fury and grabbed Ethan by the wrist. It forced him to the ground.

Ethan tried to kick the legs out from under the creature, but it kept them out of reach. He threw his body from side to side, trying to get out of the creature's killer hold. But it was no use: The alien's grip was like iron.

In desperation, Ethan grabbed onto the creature's wrist with his free hand and sunk his teeth deep into the alien flesh. The alien grimaced in pain.

Then, to my amazement, it smiled.

"Do you think you could poison us twice, fool? All you're doing is putting teeth marks in my body armor. Now, prepare to sleep . . . forever."

The alien raised back his other arm, aiming a killing blow at Ethan's neck.

Nooooo! I thought directly into the alien's mind.

The alien jerked up, confused. His head swept from side to side as he tried to find the source of the voice.

In the instant that he was distracted, Ethan twisted loose and scurried into the woods. The alien turned to pursue him, but as he did the device on his wrist began sounding a high-pitched wail.

The alien's wrist timer read "5:00." Five minutes remaining. My time was almost up.

The creature whirled toward Ethan's retreating figure. "Next time, little boy, you won't be so lucky," it shouted after him. Then, spinning on its heels, it ran back over the path toward the reservoir.

I had to warn the others. The alien was coming—and it was *mad*.

_____ Chapter 13

Again, I streamed through the woods. And the woods streamed through *me*.

It was difficult not to flinch as branches and tree trunks flashed before me and then were gone—left to eat my astral dust. My life force penetrated them as if they weren't there at all.

And suddenly I was back at the reservoir. Back outside the spaceship.

Ashley and Jack were standing directly beneath the alien craft, surrounded by its six tall, insect-like legs. They had their heads tilted back and were staring up at the underside of the ship.

Hey, guys, I thought at them. *I'm back, and I got bad news. The alien is coming. So you gotta get me out. Quick.*

"Sure," said Jack. "Just as soon as you tell us how *we* get *in*."

Use the hatchway, I transmitted.

"What hatchway?" said Ashley.

I followed her upward gaze and immediately saw the problem.

There *was* no hatchway.

The bottom of the spaceship was as smooth and featureless as a mirror. No hatchway in sight. Not even the outline of a door.

I don't understand, I said. *It has to be there. I saw it.*

"Did you see how it opens?" Ashley said. "Was there a button, or a control panel or something?"

I don't know, I answered. I was growing worried.

Ashley started pulling off her boots.

"Here, Jack. Help me up on your shoulders."

Jack interlaced his fingers, then bent over to allow Ashley to place her foot in his hands. She did, setting her hands on his shoulders for balance. He straightened, and Ashley stepped up effortlessly onto his shoulders. They performed this feat with such speed and ease that it was like watching two acrobats.

Boy, that's impressive, I thought.

"You should see me underwater," said Ashley

dryly. From atop Jack's shoulders, she was just tall enough to touch the lower surface of the spaceship.

She raised her hands above her head, placing her palms flat against the metal hull.

"Do you feel anything?" said Jack, bracing her ankles with his hands.

"Well, it's warm," she replied, sliding her hands across the slick surface. "And kind of . . . tingly."

Is there a latch or lever or something? I was trying to keep my cool, but I could feel myself starting to panic. How much time before the alien got here? Three minutes? Two?

"Nope," Ashley replied. "Not even a crack." She started pounding her fist against the alien craft. It was like hitting solid steel. It didn't even make a sound.

"Do you think it could be voice triggered?" Jack asked. "Maybe there's a special password."

A password?

"You know," said Jack. "Like 'Open Sesame' or something."

As soon as Jack said those words, a laser-white crack appeared on the silver hull, right above Ashley's head. It began to grow wider, slowly opening to reveal the hatchway beyond.

129

"I don't believe you just did that," said Ashley.

I don't think he did, I told her. *I think it means we've got company.*

Sure enough, I could hear the sound of rapid footfalls growing nearer.

The hatchway door was still sliding open.

"What do we do?" Jack asked, casting a nervous glance toward the woods. Any second now the creature would come bursting through the trees.

Hide, I thought at them. *Save yourselves.*

"But I can almost get a hold . . . ," said Ashley, reaching into the bright shaftway above her. "Maybe if I jump—"

There's no time, I said to them. *Get away.*

"She's right, Ash," said Jack. "We're sitting targets. We can't save her if we get caught, too."

Ashley frowned, biting her lip. Then she nodded. She jumped down from Jack's shoulders, landing gracefully on the ground. "Hang in there, El," she said, grabbing up her boots. "We'll be back."

Then the two of them dashed off to hide.

No sooner had they left the landing site than the alien charged into view.

Positioning himself below the hatchway, he pushed a button on his wrist device. The ramp started descending from the bright opening above.

Just as the alien was about to step on the ramp, it paused, its eye caught by something on the ground.

It had noticed Jack and Ashley's footprints in the snow, leading both to and from the spaceship.

The creature's black eyes narrowed, and it peered out across the frozen reservoir, then back into the surrounding woods. Then it glanced at the timer on its wrist.

It's trying to decide if it should follow them or not.

For a second, my astral heart leaped. A happy ending played out in my astral brain:

The alien would follow the tracks into the woods, leaving the ship open and unguarded. While it was gone, Jack and Ashley could sneak aboard, free me, and then together we could make our escape.

But the next second, my hopes were dashed.

The alien turned and walked into the ship. Soon its legs disappeared inside the glowing interior.

The ramp rose swiftly back into the hatchway. Then the hatch door began to slide shut.

Nooooo! my mind screamed. *This can't be happening.*

It was like watching the end of a movie and finding out the hero wasn't going to win.

The entire spaceship began to make an incredible humming sound. The lights on its outer rim began to light in sequence, around and around, faster and faster.

I knew what that meant.

It's going to take off, I thought. *It's going to take off with my body on board!*

Elena, are you there? Can you hear me? Jack's voice—or, rather, his mind's voice—rang loudly in my ears. I could sense him somewhere back in the woods, watching the ship, just as I was.

Jack, I thought back at him, *is that you?*

Yes, it's me. Listen to me, Elena. You have to get back in your body.

Are you crazy? I thought. *Get back on that ship with that horrible creature? Never.*

The idea was too dreadful to imagine.

Jack's right, Elena. Ashley's voice suddenly sounded in my mind. *You have to reenter your body while you still have a chance.*

Or you'll be stuck as a spirit forever, Jack added. *You said so yourself.*

132

Yeah, I thought back at them. *But at least I'd be stuck here on earth, not trapped in some UFO with that bug-eyed freakazoid.*

Besides, I added to myself, *it wouldn't be so bad, being stuck in astral form. I could float around all day. Just float and fly and be warm and feel at peace. . . .*

Elena! Snap out of it! Jack was yelling at me now. *That's not what you really want.*

Think of your mother, Ashley added. *You think she wants a ghost for a daughter?*

I did think of my mother. I thought of my mother, and then I thought of Todd Aldridge's mother.

I imagined Mom with Carol Aldridge's sad, haunted eyes.

No. I don't want that, but . . .

Then go back in your body! Ashley's mind voice ordered. *And hurry!*

Around the spaceship, a steadily rising wind whipped at the trees and blew powdery snow into the air. Then the clouds above the reservoir began to rotate, swirling together. They started funneling upward, as if being sucked by some giant vacuum.

But if I go back it will kill me! I thought.

If it was going to kill you, it would have done it

already, Ethan's mind voice stated. He had joined our telepathic conversation. *There must be some reason that it wants to keep you alive.*

Why? I said. *How can I be sure?*

You can't, Ethan answered. *But you have to take that chance.*

I knew he was right.

If I stayed behind, my human body would still be at the mercy of that hideous fiend.

If I went back, there was the chance that I could reenter my body and escape.

Besides, I wasn't totally clear on how this astral stuff worked.

What happened if my human body died? Would my astral body die, too?

I couldn't let that happen. Not without a fight.

And yet, the thought chilled me to the bottom of my soul.

I'm frightened, guys, I thought.

You can do it, they told me. *We're here for you. We'll find a way to rescue you.*

Then, with their promise ringing in my ears and the last rays of sunshine fading on the horizon, I made my way back toward the humming ship.

I floated toward the hull, felt my astral body begin to penetrate its slick metallic skin—

Then watched in shock and horror as the ship started pulling away from me. I flailed my arms but couldn't grab onto it; it slipped right through me, leaving me staring up helplessly as it shot like a missile into the sky, straight for the center of the cloud funnel.

It was leaving without me.

My *body* was leaving without me.

I flew up after it, like a stream of light.

I couldn't let it get away. I suddenly realized how important it was that I get back inside my human form.

Concentrating all my energy, I was able to gain on the retreating craft. I narrowed the distance to fifty yards . . . thirty . . . fifteen . . . ten . . .

Once again, my astral form penetrated the outer shell of the craft.

And all at once I was back in the control room.

I saw my body inside the plastic tube, its eyes closed in sleep.

At least I *hoped* it was sleep.

I rushed toward it, felt myself being sucked into it—

And suddenly everything went black.

There was utter silence . . . stillness.

Nothingness.

For a second, I panicked. I thought that I'd been too late. That I had entered a dead body.

But then I heard it.

Bmm-bmmp . . . bmm-bmmp . . . bmm-bmmp . . .

A heartbeat. *My* heartbeat. Growing louder. And stronger.

Bmm-bmmp . . . Bmm-bmmp . . . Bmm-bmmp!

And I not only heard it, but suddenly could *feel* it as well. Pulsing. Beating in my rib cage. Pumping life-giving blood through my chest, and arms, and legs.

I was back in my body!

I wish I could say it felt wonderful to have returned to human form. But it didn't. It felt awful. To trade the light, floating freedom of my astral form for a body with weight and mass and physical sensations—it was like being squeezed inside a lead suit four sizes too small. And electrified. My entire body tingled with an intense pins-and-needles sensation. I was aware of painful cramps in my legs and arms, and a bitter taste in my mouth. Just when I thought things couldn't possibly get worse, my eyes flickered open—

And things did.

Because I found myself staring straight into two jet black, evil orbs.

136

Fear washed over me like a wave of acid.

"Elena Vargas," the alien hissed from outside the plastic tube.

"Where are you taking me?" I whimpered. "What are you going to do to me?" I was sickened by the weakness in my voice. But I couldn't breathe deeply enough to give my words any force.

The alien clucked its tongue in mock dismay.

"How disappointed your father would be, to hear his daughter ask so many foolish questions." As it spoke, it raised a long, pale hand to the tube, stroking the plastic directly over my face. For once I was thankful for the thick barrier between us. "Apparently his talents aren't as developed in your tiny little brain, or you would already know the answers."

"*Tell me!*" I yelled through clenched teeth.

The alien jerked its hand away, as if I'd just bitten him. "But I see you *have* inherited your father's willpower," it stated.

It leaned in closer to me.

"I'm bringing you back where you belong," the alien said. "You must have realized that you were not meant for that world."

As it peered at me with its coal black eyes, I was overcome by a now-familiar dizzy feeling.

My mind reeled. My legs went weak. With a sudden flash, an image appeared in my mind's eye.

When my vision had passed, I stared right back into my captor's eyes. "You may have gotten me," I said with a steely calmness. "But you didn't get my friends. You failed."

"The others will be ours, in time," the alien said. It turned away from me, but not before I caught a glimpse of something—Doubt? Fear?—flicker across its horrible face.

As the spaceship hurtled toward its unknown destination, the terror that had paralyzed me was slowly replaced by a different feeling.

Hope.

I closed my eyes and tried to concentrate on the vision I'd been granted:

I had seen myself, reunited with Ethan, Ashley, and Jack . . . and others. And we were happy. Laughing.

I knew that they would come for me. I knew that they would find me. Rescue me.

It was just a matter of time.

About the Author

Chris Archer grew up in New Jersey, where he spent most of his childhood wishing he had special powers.

He now divides his time between New York City and Los Angeles, California. When Chris is not writing books and screenplays, he enjoys going to scary movies, playing piano (badly), and reading suspense novels.

He has never been to Wisconsin.

Don't miss

mindwarp™

Shape-shifter

Coming in mid-March
From MINSTREL Paperbacks